Three Deadly Days in Spain

*Three Deadly
Days
in
Spain*

Three Deadly Days in Spain

Mary Branham

SUNSTONE
PRESS

SANTA FE

Printed and bound in the United States of America. No part of this book may be reproduced in any form or by any electronic or mechanical means including information storage and retrieval systems without permission in writing from the publisher, except by a reviewer who may quote brief passages in a review.

Sunstone books may be purchased for educational, business, or sales promotional use. For information please write: Special Markets Department, Sunstone Press, P.O. Box 2321, Santa Fe, New Mexico 87504-2321.

FIRST EDITION

Library of Congress Cataloging-in-Publication Data:
Branham, Mary, 1929–
    Three deadly days in Spain / Mary Branham.—1st ed.
      p. cm.
    ISBN: 0-86534-315-2 (hardcover) ISBN: 978-1-63293-109-2 (softcover)
      1. Women detectives—Spain—Fiction. 2. Americans—Spain—Fiction.
3. Spain—Fiction. I. Title.
      CIP
PS3552.R3238 T47 2000
813' .54—dc21   00-044661

Published by   SUNSTONE PRESS
               Post Office Box 2321
               Santa Fe, NM 87504-2321 / USA
               (505) 988-4418 / orders only (800) 243-5644
               FAX (505) 988-1025
               www.sunstonepress.com

For Jim and Brenda and Vicki
who make publishing a book fun.

. . . they had an adventure, or something
that was uncommonly like one.

—*Don Quixote of La Mancha*,
Miguel de Cervantes Saavedra

"A holy relic from the seventeenth century," Sydney Reardon answered in reply to the question from the JFK security guard about what was in the ornate silver box that had just set off the alarm. At least she had thought quickly enough to not explain in detail that it was a little finger from the left hand of a priest slain during the Pueblo Revolt of 1680 in what is now New Mexico. That would have seemed absurd to the skeptical officer facing her.

"Oh?" he questioned, with that look of distrust Sydney habitually associated with law enforcement types.

The box had been given to her only minutes ago by a sister from a monastery on Long Island. Everything was in order.

"Wait," she said. "I have all the official church papers. And I have a letter to a Mother Mary Henriette in Spain. In Avila. I'm going to give the relic to her tomorrow."

Of course she had agreed to take the finger the moment Peter asked her. It seemed an exotic errand. Like many Protestants, Sydney had great interest in, and little knowledge of, things Catholic. She produced the papers.

"Mighty heavy."

She had thought the same thing and questioned it.

9

"It's the box that's heavy. And old," she told him as the nun had explained to her.

He waved her on.

In Sydney Reardon's view there are two kinds of people in the world: those who arrive at an airport more than an hour ahead for domestic flights and at least two hours before overseas departures, and those who rush the last twenty yards to make it before the doors close. Sydney was the second kind. Yes, she missed a flight now and then, but she avoided waiting. She had not cut it so close today because of meeting the nun.

She was through the entrance saying good-evening to the crew when there was the announcement: a delay. Passengers were to remain on board.

Sydney sighed. So much for waiting, she thought, as she stowed her raincoat and soft taupe carry-on overhead and settled into the aisle seat of the second row in the first-class section. The box and her big purse were tucked neatly under the seat ahead of her.

"Would you like something to drink?" the cabin attendant was asking, holding a bottle of champagne and a glass invitingly.

"I'd like Scotch—Johnny Walker Black—and water," Sydney said. "Easy on the water."

She took the first sip and sighed with pleasure. There were advantages, other than room for her long legs, to being in first class. She moved over to the empty window seat to watch the coveralled folk frolicking on the asphalt under the big aircraft. At least they seemed to be mostly playing, talking with one another and laughing. No doubt they knew what they were doing and it was vitally important to the trip ahead but she always had the illusion that they were somehow aimless, or at least directionless.

The delay was now stretching toward two hours. From what

she could see they were unloading baggage rather than loading it.

The captain walked through making pleasantries and assuring passengers that they would soon be on their way.

"They seem to be unloading luggage," Sydney commented when he paused to chat.

"You're absolutely right. We had two bags checked to Madrid and the passenger who left them did not board so we have to find them. Probably a perfectly plausible explanation but we'd rather have disgruntled people sitting here than take a chance." Smiling, he moved on.

"You dumb son-of-a-bitch. Henry, how could you of checked a suitcase with heroin in it? Didn't Ma teach you nothin'? She's kept us clean."

"Andy, in the first place she's kept us clean because she's paid thugs and killers to do the dirty jobs. She's in there sweet-talkin' those helpless old ladies. She's got us doin' the same thing."

He could hear his brother's angry breathing at the other end of the line. He was trying to cut in but Henry didn't let him.

"In the second place you and Ma have always thought I'm dumb and I've never got my fair share. Altogether I've taken in a few hundred thousand. You and Ma are way up in the millions.

"In the third place I made this deal on the side because I need money. You know Alma spends ever cent she can get her hands on. I've got kids. You and Ma ain't fair and I need cash now. The fancy studs in Europe want to snort it just like the big shots here. I saw a good chance to make something."

"That chance to make something may have fucked up everything. You tell me yourself that Ma takes care of the dirty jobs. You admit she hires killers. Believe me, she'll take care of you if she has to. You know Ma as well as I do. I don't think it would bother her much. She hates dumb."

"Don't it ever bother you that we're stealin' sick old ladies blind? Don't it bother you that Ma gets anybody killed that gets in the way so we can sell stolen diamonds? It was Grandma's wedding ring gettin' stolen that set this thing off. Think about it. When that worthless ring was stolen by somebody in that stinkin' nursing home what did Ma do? She got an idea worth millions."

"Ma's a genius."

"Ma's a thief. Just like us. And a killer. Maybe she don't kill nobody herself but she gets Hugo and those creeps that work for him to do it. How many has Ma had blown away?"

"I don't know but I notice you take the money. You ain't said a word till now about not gettin' your share. You haven't said one damn word about folks gettin' killed. Now you've got your tail over the dashboard and you're hollerin'. You make me wanna puke."

"You talk down to me all the time. You always have. You and Ma. Listen. Listen hard. I'll bring you both down. Tell her Henry ain't as dumb as she thinks. Tell her Henry is gonna sing a song she won't like to those bastards that picked me up."

"Screw you Henry. We'll get back to you after you've had a chance to sweat."

"Screw you Andy. If I don't hear from you soon—in less than an hour—you just made one hell of a big mistake."

Wincing as he heard Andy slam down the receiver, Henry looked at his watch.

He kept looking.

Thirty minutes.

Forty.

Forty-nine.

Fifty-three.

Fifty-nine minutes since his brother hung up.

Ma and Andy were not going to help him.

*   *   *   *   *

"I want to talk to somebody in charge."

The chief of security walked over to him.

"I'm in charge."

"Get somebody to take this down. You're holdin' me because I'm stupid. I checked a suitcase with heroin in it."

"So?"

"I want to make a deal. I can tell you plenty. Plenty."

"You sure you want to talk without a lawyer? Did they read you your rights?"

"I don't care about rights this minute. I'm trustin' you and that's probably another big mistake. But if you don't cross me they will."

The security boss summoned a mild-looking young man wearing thick glasses. Sitting down, he turned on a machine.

"Record this. Ready?"

"Yes, sir."

"Ready?"

"Yeah. There's somebody on that plane with ten million in stolen gems. Mostly diamonds. Some emeralds."

If it surprised the security chief he did not show it. "Who?"

"Sydney Reardon."

"Description?"

"I don't know. All I got is a name for this delivery but I know plenty more about the whole operation."

"We'll check it out. What do you want in return?"

"Protection from Edna and Andy and Hugo."

"Who are they?"

14

"Ma, and my brother, and Ma's hired jerk."

"Protection from your mother?"

"Yeah."

"Christ! Sit there. I'll check the passenger list. You keep talking."

It was a relief to be telling it all. The boy who was recording it didn't ask questions. He just watched the machine. Henry couldn't tell if he was listening. His watch kept ticking. He'd done the right thing. Ma wasn't going to call.

"You're right about a Sydney Reardon being on the airplane. Come on. You're going for more questions."

Henry followed him out to the curb where a NYPD car was waiting. A young officer got out and came around the car. The men shook hands.

"I don't know you."

"Todd Givens." He produced his ID.

"New?"

"To this detail. I've been with the department three years."

"Deliver him to Lieutenant Jarboe. I'll fax what we've got."

"Want me to take it?"

"No, I'll get it to him."

"Right."

Henry ducked his head as they doubled him into the car.

Officer Givens pulled easily out of the airport lot and into traffic. He took an exit Henry couldn't place.

"Think I've got a bad tire," he said parking at the curb.

Henry looked around, gasping as the door opened. Hugo Wolf's big bald head and massive shoulders pushed toward him. He never saw Hugo without thinking of a football game.

"You must of been a lineman," he said once.

15

"Yeah. In high school. A long time ago. That's as far as I ever got. Didn't finish there," Hugo admitted.

The hulking man settled his heavy frame onto the seat. Henry realized he had never seen Hugo without a cigarette dangling between his puffy lips, sometimes lit, sometimes not. With his tongue he shifted the cigarette from one side of his mouth to the other. Hugo's tongue was not tongue color—it was purple. When he used it to shift the cigarette it made Henry gag.

"We're not sure what you told them."

"Nothin'."

"Oh yeah, you told them some. But they're takin' you so they hope for a lot more. Too bad for them."

"I thought you was on the plane for Madrid."

"I thought you was too."

"I was but they found the heroin."

"Stupid. Why was you goin' to Madrid anyhow?"

"To make sure you did your job."

"Shit, your mamma don't trust nobody." He giggled. That terrifying, unnerving sound Henry hated.

"Why should she?"

"You're right when her own son fucked up."

In desperation Henry looked at the front seat. "Where's that cop?"

He giggled again. "You really are dumb. That cop is one of my boys. We thought if you started to talk they might send you to the big boys. He's out of here."

"Hugo I know you. I know you're gonna kill me. But what you don't know is how much I told them. I can tell you one thing. I told them plenty. It's all over."

With a doubled fist Hugo hit Henry hard enough to force him to the floor between the seats. He quickly put one heavy

16

boot on the frightened man's back to hold him down and with the other crushed his skull.

Hugo stepped out of the squad car, crossed the street and hailed a cab.

"JFK. TWA International. I'm late. Make tracks. It'll be worth it."

Sydney had been standing in the aisle to stretch her legs but for her second drink she returned to her seat. She was about to look at the biography of Saint Teresa the nun had given her when word came that they were preparing for take-off. At that moment a slim young man ambled in, tossing a khaki canvas bag into the overhead compartment and flashing a smile as he slipped past her to the window seat.

"Bourbon," he returned when the crew member offered him champagne. "On the rocks."

Sydney looked at him carefully. Beautiful was the only word. In addition to his good looks she admired his timing. She had been waiting for almost two hours. He had arrived after the delay.

He turned toward her and lifted his glass. "To our adventure."

"Adventure?"

"Whatever lies ahead."

He sampled his drink and then did something that endeared him to her at once. He opened a battered, bent, hardcover copy of *Don Quixote*.

"You like *Don Quixote*?"

"Don't you?"

"Oh yes," she answered and, smiling, added, "When I can't quite sort out what's real I always pick up the book."

"So do I." He shook his dark curly locks and ripped a long silk, multi-colored scarf from around his neck. His hands tightened around the scarf as he twisted it in front of him in intricate gyrations. "I'm mad about the Don. I've gotten to know him well only recently. I think I may have been him in some earlier incarnation." He flashed the smile and shook the curls again. The lavender, red and orange scarf settled back around his neck, dropping haphazardly over a cashmere sweater that exactly matched the lavender in the scarf. The sweater was just rumpled enough to be perfect with his off-white jeans.

Sydney Reardon was confident about style. She knew she was chic. But suddenly she felt a bit conservative. When she had dressed for the flight in wheat colored pants and a matching silk sweater with lots of good jewelry she was pleased. Pants were becoming to her trim hips and long legs and she wore them often. They were comfortable and that was an added attraction for travel. Since the accident, low heels were easier for walking and they were perfect with pants. Sydney glanced at her seatmate. She wondered if a bright scarf might have been a nice touch for her. Am I really being influenced by flashy clothes on a pretty boy, she pondered.

He was sipping his bourbon and savoring some no doubt well-remembered, oft-read, encounter of his hero.

She opened the Saint Teresa book. It was autographed. She couldn't make out the signature but no doubt it was the mother superior of the Long Island monastery. *Thank you for the merciful task you are performing.* The message went on to assure her that the prayers of the sisters were with her. Two holy bookmarks fell from the pages as she laid the book face down across her knees.

The young man by the window glanced at her as he turned a page. "Wow. It's incredible. Two of my favorite characters from literature on the same aisle."

"Characters from literature?"

"Or figures from history," he returned.

Sydney pointed to his book. "I've always had trouble thinking of Don Quixote as fictional," she confided.

"So have I. On the other hand, Teresa of Avila doesn't seem quite real."

"I don't know all that much about her. I was intrigued by her when I read Phyllis McGingley's *Saint Watching* years ago and once when I was stopping in Avila I looked her up in the *Britannica*.

"Is there a person on earth who can look for something in an encyclopedia and not read whatever's on either side? I learned that teredo is a genus of highly specialized wormlike bivalve mollusks belonging to a family commonly known as shipworms.

"Terence, after Plautus, was the greatest Roman writer of comedy. When, about 150 B.C.?

"I tried to stop after Teresa but there was Teresina, capital of the state of Piauí, Brazil.

"And Albert Payson Terhune, novelist and short story writer, famous for his stories about dogs. I'm sure you knew about the dog stories but I'll wager you didn't know that his mother wrote romantic novels under the pen name of Marion Harland. It's all there in the *Britannica*."

The young man grinned. "Did you ever get around to reading about Saint Teresa?"

"Oh yes. TERESA, SAINT, of Avila, 1515-1582. I learned

that she had seven brothers who became colonial officials in South America and that her two sisters married and lived in Spain.

"At twenty-one she went to the Carmelite convent in Avila as a novice. After a couple of years her health failed and she was an invalid for three years. When she recovered she said that, on the one hand God was calling her, on the other, she was following the spirit of the world. One day, I don't remember how long but a good while, she was praying and her heart was touched and she began a new prayerful life. Her dream was to live the contemplative life of the cloister, but her superiors had other plans. In the next two decades she established more than a dozen convents around Spain.

"In spite of her frail health she traveled all the time. Imagine what that was like in sixteenth-century Spain. She died en route from Burgos to Avila. Her writings have lasted over the centuries. They're still best sellers."

Her listener was thoughtful. "I believe the two of them, Don Q. and Teresa, had a lot in common."

"What?"

"Well, they both traipsed all over the country all the time. Not often under the most favorable circumstances."

"And they did unlikely things," Sydney added. "For instance, Teresa taught her nuns to dance for joy in the cloisters."

"And Don Quixote did nothing but unlikely things. Moderation was certainly not the secret for either of them.

"We agree on Teresa and Quixote," he offered as they enjoyed their drinks. "And we don't prefer champagne. We should get better acquainted. It's a pretty long flight. I'm Ben Harris."

"Sydney Reardon."

"I thought you were a man."

"I beg your pardon."

21

"I mean, I think of Sydney as a man's name," he added quickly.

"Sydney is my mother's family name. I was not born in the South but my heritage is southern. It happens fairly often. If the first-born is not a boy then girls are sometimes given family names. Actually, I've always rather liked my name."

"I like it too," Ben Harris agreed. "And I'm glad to meet you."

They touched glasses.

"I've been in Washington, learning to be a PI."

"A PI? Private investigators really use that term? Not just on television?"

"Well, I do. Yes."

"Why on earth would you want to be a PI?"

He chuckled. "Wow. I don't know. In books and movies, and on television, they lead exciting lives, don't they?"

Sydney looked at him intently, almost staring. He certainly didn't seem the PI type. Frivolous young man. Just the kind she liked. Anyhow, not really her concern. His enthusiasm was appealing and what better did she have to do than listen to the story of his young life.

"While I was absorbing all that law and order I ran down to Annapolis and enrolled in the Graduate Institute at St. John's College. It took a while but I got a master's on the side. Liberal arts, reading Great Books, that stuff they're known for. It was exciting. That's where I got to really know Don Quixote."

"Interesting. I'm going to Salamanca to visit a friend who used to be a tutor at St. John's—in Santa Fe."

"Hmm."

"Peter Farber. Ever hear of him?"

"No, but I've never been to the New Mexico campus. I was in Annapolis only for classes. Don't know anyone much there."

"Dinner will be along shortly." The attendant was smiling over them, offering replenished drinks.

Sydney stepped into the aisle. "I'm going to take a walk before dinner." She held onto the back of the seat, hesitating before she moved.

"Are you all right?" Ben Harris started to get up from his seat.

"I'm fine, really. I had an accident a few years ago and it's a bit difficult to get moving when I sit for too long. You were lucky to have arrived as we were ready for take-off. I had the misfortune of waiting a couple of hours."

Dinner was served just as Sydney returned to her seat.

They enjoyed acceptable little steaks. And Rioja. Quite a lot of it.

He went on with his personal chronicle. By the time they were finishing their wine Sydney knew that Ben Harris was barely twenty-four, an only child with a doting and apparently rich mother who was sometimes in California but more often in France. Betsy he called her. Sounded as if she financed anything he fancied. He was now on his way to follow in the footsteps of his hero, Don Quixote.

"I think my training as an investigator will be helpful with research for the play I'm going to write. There's one of the adventures that will make a great one-act play. It's the one where Don Q. and Sancho. . . ." he stopped abruptly. "I can't tell you which one.

"Why ever not?"

"I don't know." He was suddenly shy. "For some reason I'm superstitious about discussing it."

"I understand that. I'm the most superstitious person you'll ever meet."

"You are? You don't look the type."

"Looks are often deceiving."

"Why are you superstitious? Or how? Give me an example."

She laughed. "I've enjoyed our drinks and the wine but I haven't had nearly enough to tell all." Steering him away from the subject, Sydney turned back to his play. "Once upon a time I was an actress. I'd love to hear about this drama you're going to write."

"Can't tell you now. And I'm not surprised you were an actress. You seem dramatic."

"What's that supposed to mean?" she asked, laughing.

"Oh, I don't know. You're stunning looking. You have a beautiful voice and a wonderful throaty laugh. A brilliant smile. You don't seem like just folks."

Sydney smiled the wide smile that revealed perfect white teeth in a too big mouth. One of her most appealing features Townie used to say. "I take it all that's meant to be complimentary."

"Sure. Are you acting now?"

"No. I gave it up some years ago. I was too old to be an ingenue and while I was pretty sparkly in some roles I was not talented enough to be a leading lady. I decided to quit before the spark was gone."

"Don't you miss the theatre?"

"Not really. I became a decorator and that pretty much took the place of being on stage. I've always had a knack for putting chairs and lamps and tables together, and hanging paintings on a wall. Once I learned the basics I was really good."

"So that's what you do now?"

"I've segued into 'doing' as it is called, houses. You tell

me you want to recreate a colonial gem from Oaxaca or a farmhouse from Tuscany and I take care of it; from finding an architect, to antique doors, to folk art, I'm your girl."

"Wow. Sounds great. Are you going to Salamanca on a project?"

"No. I'm going to visit a friend. I'm picking up a car at the airport, stopping overnight in Avila, and then on to Salamanca for a week of being a tourist."

"I've always thought I'd like to see Avila. Do you have friends there?"

"No. I'm actually delivering a seventeenth century relic."

"A seventeenth century relic! How bizarre."

"I don't see it as bizarre at all." She was defensive. "I think of it as a gesture of kindness." How pompous and self satisfied that sounds, she thought. There was no reason to explain the circumstances to this stranger but she did. "I was going to stop over in Avila because I like the town so much. The Parador Raimundo de Borgona is a favorite of mine. I love to walk around *inside* the walls. I'm terrified of heights but I adore the little streets below. Peter, my friend, asked me if I'd bring the relic. It seemed a perfectly reasonable task and I must say it sounded pretty exciting. I was glad to say yes. You think that's bizarre?"

."I'm sorry. I was just surprised. It seems such an unlikely thing to be doing. Forgive me. Where do you go from Salamanca?"

He was trying to bring the conversation back to airplane pleasantries.

"To Lisbon for a folk art fair."

"Buying?"

"Perhaps, though I specialize mostly in Mexican work, and some Italian. Then home."

"Where's home?"

"New Mexico. Santa Fe. You said you've never been there. I think you'd like it."

"There was a shop in my neighborhood in Washington where they had those turquoise coyotes and all of whatever is Santa Fe style."

"Well, not everything in town is that precious." He was making her defensive again. She was beginning to decide she did not like him at all. "It's really a marvelous place to live. Lots of music, history, small, wonderful climate, good restaurants."

"How long have you lived there?"

"Goodness. More than three years."

"And before that?"

"Different places. New York. London. I suppose my roots are in London except for Santa Fe. I still have a flat there. Not really a flat—three rooms in a funny little old hotel. A great location. In Mayfair. I first went there with my grandmother when I was seven. She kept the place all her life. I've kept it since." She hesitated and then added, more to herself than to Ben Harris, "I haven't spent much time there recently. Until now I hadn't voiced it but I feel more and more that Santa Fe is home. I moved there because of my husband. Now I feel like a native. I love it."

"What does your husband do?"

"He's dead."

"I'm sorry. I seem to be saying all the wrong things."

Both fell silent for a moment. Following a few desultory remarks they returned to their books.

After being amused by Ben's telling all about himself she had rambled on too. Maybe too much. But she hadn't told him about her superstitions. And, she hadn't gone into detail about John's accident. It sounded so fatuous when she explained that he walked out on a Sunday morning to pick up the *New York*

26

Times at La Fonda and was struck by a woman rushing with her three little girls so they wouldn't be late for the last mass at the cathedral.

They were late for mass.

And John was dead.

She was just now able to think of him with more fondness and amusement and less overwhelming loss and sadness, she realized. For a few minutes she dozed as she thought about their trip together to Spain. Then she was awake again. She never slept well on airplanes so by the time the cabin attendant raised the shades, she had read most of the book about Saint Teresa.

Sydney was definitely not a morning person. She wandered, still a little dazed by the first light, to the restroom.

When she returned her aisle-mate was enjoying a Bloody Mary.

"Join me?"

"No thanks." She remembered the Black Label and the Rioja and thought better of it.

The sun was just above the horizon. There was not a cloud in the sky. Without warning the huge aircraft dropped through a hole.

"Jesus," Sydney muttered as she wiped the Bloody Mary off her chin, her silk sweater and her pale slacks. She looked as if she had been mortally wounded.

The captain apologized and reassured the passengers.

The liquid from Ben's drink had all been flung her way. He was untouched. He apologized, looking wistfully at the empty glass.

Trying to soothe them both, the attendant did her best to sop up the bright liquid with a towel.

The plane droned on as if nothing had happened.

"We are about to begin our final descent for landing in Madrid," a practiced, bland voice announced. "Please return to your seats." An equally undistinguished voice was repeating the message in Spanish.

Once they were on the ground Sydney ignored the request that passengers remain in their seats until the aircraft had come to a halt at the gate. She fetched her purse from the floor and placed the box inside. Outside it was a warm, sunny morning but she donned the raincoat to cover the tomato juice stains. Hastily pulling her bag from the overhead compartment and calling farewell to Ben who was dozing, she moved purposefully forward.

The Spanish customs people showed no interest in her. She didn't mention the bag of things for Peter that she had checked. There was no time to wait now. It would have to be sent to Salamanca. The sister who gave her the relic said that Mother Mary Henriette would be expecting her at 11:30. It was not quite 9:00 but how long to get the car and move out of city traffic?

Santiago Farber leaned against the wall across from the rental car desk watching over the top of his newspaper for Sydney Reardon. He was sure to recognize her. He had the photograph they had faxed and God knows his father had described her often enough so he didn't really need a picture.

"She's tall, model-thin," his father, Peter, had said. "I held my breath the first time I saw her. When she smiled at me my knees went weak."

That made Santiago chuckle. His father was a man of such few words that it was amusing to hear him rave about a woman, especially his best friend's wife. The thought of his father being weak-kneed over a woman was beyond imagination. She must be special.

He really hated the idea of killing her. Over the years he had become adept at ending a life but this would be personal. In some perverse way it had pleased Hugo to give him the assignment.

It had been easy for Santiago to get Papá to ask her to bring the 'relic.' Equally easy for Papá to convince Sydney. Santiago shook his head in puzzlement. It never ceased to amaze him that those who lived within the law were so gullible. Even his father who had fought in the civil war here, which should have been enough to disillusion him early on. After being on this planet almost eighty years Papá still bought the whole story. How much he loved his father. How much he hated killing Sydney.

"Why kill her?" Santiago had asked Hugo Wolf. "All I need to do is get the stones."

"She's smart. She's got connections. She'll ask questions if they're stolen. Kill her. Like I told you. Or. . . ." Hugo's voice trailed off.

Standing there, waiting for her to go for the car, he began to sweat. Just thinking about Hugo reminded him of the first time he had worked for him. And failed. Hugo had backed him against a warm stone wall on a late summer afternoon.

"Stand there, *Mierda de Pollo*," he ordered.

Little Chicken Shit. The only Spanish words Hugo ever used.

Hugo had slapped him hard across the mouth. When Santiago whimpered he took out a gun. With the tip of his fat tongue he rolled the ever-present cigarette from one corner of his mouth to the other.

"This is a Colt Single-Action Army. Old but good. Made in the US of A." Hugo regarded the gun with affection. "It is not fast. Fast is not important. They are fast." He threw a thumb over his shoulder to the two men with semi-automatics. "Don't pay no attention to them. Pay attention to me."

He had giggled which was surprising for a man so bulky. To this day Santiago heard that giggle in a nightmare before a job like this one. Hugo had placed a careful shot between his feet and went on talking around the cigarette. Santiago trembled. The next shot was to the left.

Tears streamed down Santiago's cheeks. "Please," he whispered, "kill me." Sobbing, he had huddled closer to the wall.

Hugo had giggled again, shot him in the foot, and walked away.

Santiago would always drag that foot but he had learned to do what was needed. He had never failed again. And, he had a dream. One day he would kill Hugo Wolf. In a reckless moment he had told the big man. Wolf had just looked at him and giggled.

Sydney Reardon was now talking with the car rental clerk in Spanish. In record time she had signed papers and a young man wearing a smart jacket decorated with the agency logo was leading her to a car. She was chatting with him, smiling easily.

". . . she smiled, no doubt,
Whene'er I passed her; but who passed without
Much the same smile? This grew; I gave commands;
Then all smiles stopped together."

Why should she remind him of those lines from Browning? What was it? *My Last Duchess*. One of his father's favorites. That was his job today. To make sure that all smiles stopped.

He followed her out to the car park, waiting patiently as she stowed a bag, a raincoat, and her purse, in the back seat. Handing the attendant a tip, she smiled and waved and then pulled skillfully into traffic.

There was a curve just after the tunnel. To force a car off the road there would be easy. The view was clear in both directions. He slipped on first one expensive black glove and then the other. If there was any chance that she was still alive it should not be difficult to help her out of the car and. . . .

There might be cars following, or coming toward them, and that could be something of a problem. There would be other opportunities. Hugo had taught him that. If you are patient there

31

is always another opportunity. Be alert and prepared. He would be ready when the right moment came.

"I don't want to kill her," he said aloud.

"*Mierda de Pollo*." He could hear Hugo's words. "That's what I pay you to do."

Paid him well.

He let two cars get between them before he guided the Porsche into the street.

The Guadarrama Mountains rose ahead, majestic in the morning sun. Sydney glanced at the diamond watch on her wrist. Wearing it was even more fun now that it was paid for. She was making good time she thought, passing the turn-off to El Escorial. There was usually no distinction between the village and the monastery. In travel brochures there did not seem to be a need to identify it as *Real Monasterio de San Lorenzo de El Escorial.* In glowing terms they simply described an outing from Madrid as a visit to El Escorial. If she were not in such a hurry she would have taken the road for a look at the great bleak but intriguing building and stopped for coffee in the little place she had discovered years ago with Townie.

"An austere little place next to that austere big place," he described the café to friends. He didn't much like Spain, or thought he didn't, but he went there twice with her because she loved it. And he encouraged her to go on her own several times. How like him to pamper her.

In spite of himself Townie had been intrigued by the royal pantheon where most Spanish sovereigns since Charles V were buried. Alfonso XIII who died in this century was missing. Why? Of course she had to pursue that trivia question. Since he had been forced to leave Spain in 1931 it made sense that he is still "temporarily" resting in Rome where he died a decade later.

Townie hadn't agreed that the monastery was one of the handsomest religious establishments in the world but he began to conjure a drama when he learned of the Rotting Room where the royal remains were placed for a couple of decades to shrink so they'd fit the ornate crypts. The theatricality of it all brought out the producer in him and he could envision a macabre drama.

John had been in Spain with her only once. He was taken with everything about the country and they had planned to return. He had been fascinated by the immensity of the Escorial and the art collection. He was awed by the library founded by Philip II and the thought that it housed 4,000 manuscripts and more than 40,000 printed books. Since the manuscript of the *Life*, in Saint Teresa's own handwriting, was in the Escorial he would have found it worth note that she was going to Avila to deliver a relic.

But Pearson had never been to Spain. They had dreamed of travel as the young do when it is out of the question. They had been busy and in love so it didn't really matter. They had loads of time. They would have had time for travel if it hadn't been for Vietnam.

How different Pearson and Townie and John were. And yet she loved them equally. One had been gone such a short time, and one not such a long time. The other had been dead what now seemed a long, long time.

Sydney returned from her reverie to pass a slow moving truck.

Valle de los Caidos, the sign said. Valley of the Fallen, and she was reminded of Peter. Must be my day for nostalgia, she thought. Peter had gone to Spain when he was just a boy, to fight in the civil war, and had stayed on for years. He didn't talk about

34

his experiences other than a reference now and then to Franco as "that old bastard." But then Peter didn't indulge in war stories. He never fought in another war. It was hard to think of quiet Peter killing.

When he retired from St. John's he moved immediately to Salamanca and began urging her to visit. He was enjoying every class at the university and every minute exploring the old city. He wanted to share his discoveries with her. In his late seventies, Peter was still one of the most vital and curious men she could think of. At the same time he was detached, an observer, not really a participant.

John had considered Peter his closest friend. She had known him only a short time but she had come to love him too. She recalled the first night they met when Peter joined John and her at The Palace for his birthday.

He had seemed to fill the doorway as he hesitated, trying to spot them. Lino appeared instantly and led him to their booth. Peter was six-feet-five and looked to be mostly legs. He leaned forward a bit as he walked and watching him she had the feeling he was on stilts.

John had stood and moved toward him. They had embraced. He had hugged her too, which was out of character John had explained later. He was so undemonstrative. Withdrawn, most people thought. The rapport between Peter and her had been instant. He had talked freely to Sydney. John had marveled because he said Peter did only short-speak except in seminar where words flowed and he was brilliant.

Sydney slowed as she approached a line of cars. Traffic had stopped at the mouth of the tunnel. She braked behind the car ahead and tapped her fingers impatiently on the steering wheel as she waited for the impasse to break. Fiddling with the radio she found a station with classical music. Jacqueline du Pré was just finishing the Elgar cello concerto that she loved. Did du Pré play with more passion than almost anyone or was it because of her tragedy that we think she did?

"Siento mucho la tardanza," the uniformed officer said as he paused beside each car. *"Un accidente de descuido adentro."*

She was sorry for the delay too. If there was an accident inside the tunnel, even a slight one as he described, there might be quite a wait.

She glanced in the mirror at the shiny black Porsche behind her. Sydney loved fancy cars but she really preferred old ones. The driver of that car was drumming his fingers on the wheel too. He was wearing gloves, she noticed. Must be a serious driver.

When they finally emerged from the tunnel and tried to sort themselves out Sydney knew she was going to be quite late. If she remembered correctly, there was a truck stop somewhere nearby. There, ahead. She pulled out of the line of traffic and turned into the lot.

"Siento mucho, Señora. El telefono no funciona."

It couldn't be out of order.

But it was.

Coming in from Madrid Avila was always a disappointment. Probably to everyone. Why did you expect the walls to be spectacular from a distance on all sides? She'd stop tomorrow on the road to Salamanca for that dramatic view.

Fortunately she knew the route to the parador.

"I need to have you make a call at once. Mother Mary Henriette was expecting me more than an hour ago." She handed the concierge a slip of paper with the number.

The answer was immediate.

He spoke and after listening for a moment, turned to Sydney. "Mother is at prayers."

She explained the delay and he repeated her words.

"Mother Mary Henriette will see you at eleven o'clock tomorrow morning," he said as he hung up. He had felt no need to ask if that would be agreeable.

"A cleaners?" Sydney said to the man carrying her bag. He looked at her questioningly.

"*Una tintorería?*"

"*No. No. Hasta el Lunes.*"

No cleaners open until Monday. By then the tomato juice on her sweater and pants would be permanent.

"*Gracias.*"

The room was just the one she had requested. The narrow balcony with the railing high enough so she wouldn't mind having the glass doors ajar. As soon as the bellman opened the windows she looked expectantly toward the rooftop across the way. The stork's nest was still there, clinging to the slate roof beside the chimney, as it had been all these years.

When the man left Sydney moved her bag from the luggage stand onto the bed. Unpack, change clothes, have lunch. Then she'd ring Peter and explain that she couldn't go to the monastery until late tomorrow morning so she would not reach Salamanca until sometime in the afternoon. She unzipped the bag.

A passport fell out.

Mine is in my purse.

She opened the document. Ben Harris looked back at her, an edge of his beautiful face embossed by a government stamp.

It was a few seconds before she realized that in her haste she had grabbed the wrong bag from the overhead compartment.

She laid out the contents:

Shirts

Pants

A sweater

Socks

Scarves

Boxer shorts. Not the kind Pearson or Townie or John, or any other man she had seen in underwear, would pack for a trip. These were silk, soft and sensuous. A pair, black background, had red dots on one side, stripes on the other. There was a pair with wide green stripes on a yellow background. A pair covered with flowers—wonderful orange poppies. She couldn't imagine any of the men in her life, lovers or husbands, or relatives, wearing anything but fine-grade cotton, white probably, or pale blue. Sydney felt dated and laughed as she went on through the contents of the bag.

A shaving kit

A flask of bourbon

Shoes

At the bottom, a wad of bills:

  hundreds

  fifties

  twenties

She counted. And counted.

"Jesus!" Fifty thousand dollars.

How do I find Ben Harris? she tried to decide.

He had told her quite a lot about himself though nothing about where he was going except to follow Don Quixote.

He knows where I'll be. He'll find me. I can count on it. He'll come looking for his money and his passport even if the clothes aren't all that important. Or are they? she wondered.

She chose the poppy-decorated underwear and selected a pair of fawn slacks, a yellow shirt, a paisley scarf. And the taupe flats she had worn on the flight. His shoes were out of the question but everything else looked quite good she observed as she checked in the mirror. Glad she was five-feet-ten and he was not six-feet-six. Quite comfortable too.

Lunch.

Then call Peter.

After siesta go shopping for something to tide over until Ben appeared and they could exchange luggage.

First, leave all that money and the relic in the hotel safe. Sydney hardly ever gave a thought to theft. She left jewelry around all the time but then it was insured if not paid for. She did remember that her Santa Fe neighbors had *everything* removed from the trunk of their car last year while they wandered through a castle in Portugal.

She could not ever think of the name of that little restaurant but she knew exactly how to find it. Literally a hole in the wall. She had lunched there with Townie on their first stop in Avila and had returned four or five times over the years.

Upstairs it was sunny, and at this hour quiet. She leaned back in her chair and sipped Tío Pepe.

"Una fritada de camarones." She studied the menu. *"Y una ensalada de verduras, por favor."*

Exactly what she craved. A shrimp omelet, a salad and good sherry.

Where is Ben Harris at this moment? Wherever he is he must be thinking about his fifty thousand and his passport. He'll try to call. If he has as much trouble reaching me as I had trying to get through he'll be frustrated.

Back to the parador to talk with Peter before going shopping.

He answered on the first ring.

"Peter, it's Sydney."

"Where are you? How are you?"

One of Peter's amusing characteristics was his straightforward way of questioning. She smiled. "I'm fine. But I'm in Avila longer than I anticipated. I was delayed and Mother Mary Henriette can't see me until almost noon tomorrow. I'll probably have lunch here and be later getting to you than I expected. How do I find you?"

"Meet me in the Plaza Mayor. Between four and five."

"Great. Where?"

"My favorite place is on the left. Green chairs, green cloths."

"Your left or stage left?"

"Stage left if you stop below and walk up, and that's the best approach. I'll show you later where to park near my place. Santiago will be with me."

40

He always referred to his son as Santiago, never calling the boy James or Jim or Jamie.

Boy? He had to be well into his fifties. It would be interesting to meet him after hearing about him from Peter.

"I'm looking forward to seeing you both. Tomorrow."

"Good. Trip all right, except for the delay?"

"I've had a mix-up in luggage and I'm going out now to buy some things to wear until it's all straightened out. But, yes, a pleasant journey."

It hadn't actually been all that pleasant with the long delay and the Bloody Mary incident, but it occurred to her that it had been quite all right because of Ben Harris. She had forgiven him for asking awkward questions. What an attractive young man.

The shops were just re-opening when she walked out into the May sunshine. Siesta was such a civilized custom. She could easily learn to enjoy it if she lived long in a country where it was a ritual. There had not been time for a rest today but there would be in Salamanca. There never seemed to be time in Mexico because she was always looking at doors and fabric every minute shops were open and she used the break to make lists and notes. For a whole week in San Gimignano she'd sat in the shade every afternoon reading. She had always felt she was truly on holiday in Italy.

"Demasiado corto."

She looked ridiculous in the skirt well above her knees. The pants she'd tried on missed her ankles by several inches. This was the third shop. Most Spanish women were just not five-feet-ten. She would be much more presentable in Ben's slacks and shirts until they sorted out the luggage.

It took a long time to wander back to the parador with several pauses to look in store windows. She walked out through the Gate of the Alcazar and turned around to look back and imagine how formidable it must have seemed to invaders and how inviting to Saint Teresa when she returned from one of her arduous journeys. It was cool and shadows were lengthening in the narrow streets.

Have a drink in the hotel bar, an early supper even though she'd be eating alone, and to bed to make up for the wakeful night on the airplane.

Ben Harris parked his rental car beside a sleek black Porsche in the parador lot. Nice. That would be the perfect car for a PI. Betsy had said she was going to give him a new car for his birthday. A 911 would be fine.

"Please ring Mrs. Reardon."

"She went out a few minutes ago."

"Thanks. I'll call later. Can you give me her room number?"

"Of course."

Not like at home where it took all sorts of tricks to get that information. Ben walked outside and then hesitated. Why not go up to Sydney's room? See if that little gadget he got in PI school really would open a door. Go in, take a shower, put on fresh clothes. He grinned thinking how surprised she'd be if she returned and found him there. Not too surprised considering she had his passport and money as well as his clothes.

Halfway up the stairs he thought he should have brought her bag from the car. No matter, he'd get it later.

Ben leaned over to insert the magic opener in the lock. Voices inside. As he was straightening to look to make sure he had the right room the knob turned. He sauntered away and took several steps before looking around.

Two men were headed toward the steps he had just climbed, a bulky, beefy, bald man and a slighter one who limped. Through a hall window he watched them approach the Porsche. An innocuous blue sedan pulled up beside. He bounded down the stairs and hurried to his car.

What were they doing in Sydney's room? They didn't appear to be carrying anything.

He kept the cars in sight, not following close enough to be noticed.

They stopped in a grove of trees near the wall.

Ben parked and moved into the trees, keeping out of sight of the men who had emerged from the cars. He made himself as small as he could, slipping from tree to tree.

A man holding a semi-automatic stayed by the sedan. The other two were walking toward his hiding place while a third followed.

"You let her get to Avila?

"You let her get to the parador?

"Where the hell are the stones?"

The heavy man did not raise his voice or wait for an answer. Between questions he puffed on a cigarette.

They had passed him and he couldn't hear but he could see the big, bald one still talking. He motioned with a hand that was covered by a raincoat. The one with a limp walked ahead of him to a tower and they began to climb. Ben glanced around and was satisfied that the trees sheltered him from the gunman near the car. He had just reached the bottom step when there was an eerie giggle. A huge hand reached out and grabbed the game leg of the man in front of him. He gave a strangled scream as he pitched over the edge.

"No!" Ben shouted.

They were shooting at him from two directions. He dived into cover, flattening himself on the ground.

"Shit. There's somebody there."

Heavy footsteps were coming his way. The sound of running feet was followed by laughter. Ben moved the foliage aside and saw half a dozen boys tossing a ball back and forth, talking and laughing as they trotted up the path.

"Come on," the big man ordered.

The boys ran past Ben.

He waited until he heard the sound of engines and a rush of wheels. They must be gone. Wait a little longer, he cautioned himself.

No sound.

He stood up. There was a hot flash of pain in his head and the world went black.

"Christ, it takes her long enough to eat."

Hugo Wolf and Fernando Torres were sitting across from the corner table in the bar where Sydney was enjoying dinner. She had begun with Scotch and spent a good deal of time choosing between pork and fish and then selecting a wine. She was now sipping champagne.

Wolf leaned forward, resting his huge arms on the table. While watching Sydney he had also been watching Torres. It made him nervous when he worked with somebody new. This guy was recommended to Edna last year. When Santiago had to be replaced he thought of him. All they knew was hearsay. He was supposed to be fast with a gun and good with his fists. Torres had been talking to him and he hadn't been listening.

"What?"

"Does she still have the diamonds? You said you were in her room and you did not find them."

"Right."

"Nothing?"

"Not a thing."

"Why are you so certain we will get the diamonds if we

46

follow her to her room? Perhaps she does not now have them. Perhaps she has, as they say, given you the slip."

"Don't smart ass me. She's got 'em. Or she knows who's got 'em." Hugo struck a match to the dead cigarette dangling from the corner of his mouth. "We'll get 'em. You can count on it."

By the cut of the suit Fernando was a damn dandy. He had beauty shop nails. His English was good like he'd been to school a long time.

"Can I count on you? I think you're too pretty to get your hands dirty or muss up your clothes."

"You can count on me. I'm good with my hands. I have a closet full of well pressed suits."

His smile was cocky. Hugo didn't like him.

"And I am careful and intelligent."

"We'll see."

Sydney chatted with the waiter while she signed the bill. Hugo fidgeted. Finally she started toward her room.

The men followed, far enough behind to not be obvious but near enough to close the gap as she approached her door.

Fernando put out a hand. "Stop."

A stocky man, dressed in dark pants, a black shirt and cowboy boots, was walking along the hall just beyond Sydney's door.

"He is a cop," Fernando whispered. "He is thought to be smart and dangerous."

"Does he know you?"

"I do not think so." He motioned Hugo back as Sydney unlocked her door and disappeared inside.

"You told me you're clean. I don't like to be lied to. You got a record?"

"No. I am clean as you say. However the police have questioned me once or twice. This one is from Madrid. I do not think he knows me but why chance it?"

Hugo fingered the gun stuck in the belt of his pants. "See if he's still there."

"He is still there."

"It would be easy for the two of us to take him."

"I told you that I am careful. And intelligent. I do not wish to kill a police officer in the well lighted corridor of a hotel."

"Okay. Okay. I always tell my boys to be patient. There are plenty of chances if you're ready. We'll be ready for her tomorrow."

The dining room was not crowded on Sunday morning and Sydney easily found a place by the window.

The great table in the center of the room was, as always, laden with fruit, bread, cereal, jellies, ham, cheese and sweets.

She was rested and looking forward to the drive to Salamanca, seeing Peter, and meeting Santiago. The visit to the monastery shouldn't take long. Perhaps she'd have lunch in Salamanca rather than here.

Sydney glanced at her watch. Plenty of time to linger over breakfast and the paper. The coffee was hot and strong and she always loved to puzzle over stories in foreign newspapers. Savoring a bite of melon she folded the front page in half. Delicious!

EL CUERPO DE UN AMERICANO HALLADO EN AVILA

Body of an American found here? She looked at the story with interest. Pictures in papers outside the U.S. are even more graphic than ours, she mused as she tried the *pan dulce*. The dark blob that must be a body was only partially covered. The writing was florid and the opening paragraph melodramatic.

Suddenly the name Ben Harris leapt out at her.

"Oh Jesus," she breathed. She leaned her head on her hands for a moment trying to clear it so the words would make sense.

"*La cuenta, por favor. Me estoy sintiendo mal,*" she said to a waiter passing by. She was indeed feeling ill. So ill she might faint. Her Spanish was pretty good but she couldn't read fast enough.

She motioned to the *maitre d'*. "Can you read this story in English for me?" He looked a bit puzzled but nodded. "Please. Who was he?"

"Ben Harris. An American. He fell."

"How do they know?"

"He was carrying a credit card from the United States. He was wearing only—how do you say it—pantyhose."

"Pantyhose! And they identified him from a credit card? How?"

"He fell from the wall. Or was pushed."

"Fell? Or was pushed? Anything else?"

He skimmed the rest of the story. "No. They are seeking clues."

"Does it say whether it's the police here or from Madrid?"

"Perhaps both." He ran a finger along the last paragraph. "Nothing more."

The waiter returned with her check. "*Se siente mejor?*"

Assuring him that she was not feeling better, Sydney signed the bill and somehow managed to walk out of the dining room.

"There's that bastard of a cop that was at the hotel last night."

The two men were just closing in on Sydney when Hugo noticed a boot visible by the back wheel of a car parked near hers.

"Where?"

"Keep walkin' and talkin'," Hugo said.

As they strolled Sydney drove out of the car park without a glance toward them.

The cop followed quickly.

"You take care of him. That car." Hugo tossed Torres keys to the sedan. "I'll take the Porsche and I'll get her."

When Sydney pulled into the neatly manicured parking area at the monastery she was still dazed by news of Ben Harris' death.

The man she had noticed last night in the hall near her room was puttering in a well-tended flowerbed at the end of the ancient, vine-covered walls. He was wearing the same black shirt and, oddly enough, cowboy boots. When she saw him before she had thought he was a long way from U.S. ranching country. He seemed a little sinister then and seeing him again made her uncomfortable. I really am undone by Ben's accident, she thought. Accident?

She tugged at the rope hanging from a bell beside the massive door. The sound of the clapper was startling in the morning quiet.

The door groaned but swung easily on strong hinges. "Good morning. Señora Reardon?" inquired the brown clad figure facing her through the doorway.

"Yes. Good morning."

"This way please. Mother is expecting you." The sister was old but she moved resolutely into the courtyard.

Cloistered orders were an enigma to Sydney. The thought of contemplation and meditation was attractive on the one hand but being completely secluded would not suit her temperament she was sure. If she were a Carmelite she'd want to be an extern sister like the one she was following so she could talk with outsiders and do errands in town.

I really am a frivolous soul she chided herself, being distracted with such thoughts when I'm upset over Ben and delivering a holy relic. It had always been an escape at bad times, the ability to imagine herself in different roles. Maude was her oldest friend and she claimed Sydney did that when they were at school.

"It was the actress in you even then," Maude had remembered. "If you hadn't studied for a quiz or were frustrated over a boy you had a crush on you'd just escape into some role." Of course Maude had attributed most of Sydney's idiosyncrasies to being an actress or, in those early days, dreaming of being an actress.

Some truth in it, Sydney now admitted to herself.

They had crossed the courtyard. The sister opened a door

and motioned for her to enter. It was cool in the room, and dim. The only light came through a small window high in the wall. The wide floor boards creaked as she stepped forward.

"*Buenos días.*"

Sydney looked toward the voice and could just make out a shadowy figure seated behind a wrought iron screen. "*Buenos días.*"

"*Sientese, por favor,*" Mother Mary Henriette said.

"*Gracias.*" Sydney sat down as she had been invited. Those in religious orders were always so calm and quiet but somehow authoritarian. On her few visits with Mother Rose Teresa at the Carmelite Monastery in Santa Fe she had felt the same compulsion to comply immediately, she remembered.

"Señor Carlos at the parador told us that you have brought a relic. Who was the martyr?" She had moved effortlessly to English with just a trace of an accent.

"I think it was a priest. I don't know." Sydney hesitated, realizing she hadn't really given it much thought.

"Tell me. How is it that you have this relic?"

"I have a friend who lives in Salamanca. He teaches at the university. Peter Farber. Do you know him?"

"No, but I have heard of him. He is a renowned scholar."

"Yes. Well, he called me early in the week. In Santa Fe. He asked if I would bring the relic."

"From Santa Fe? In New Mexico?"

"No. From a monastery on Long Island."

"And you agreed?"

"Yes."

Sydney extracted the ornate metal box from her large leather purse. "Here. It was given to me at the airport in New York by a nun." She started to hand the box to Mother Mary

53

Henriette and realized that she couldn't because of the grill. "I have all of the official church papers."

"Just there. Place it on the turn." The mother superior pointed to a turnstile in the corner. "Thank you for your most considerate act of kindness. Our prayers will be with you."

She was being dismissed. Sydney rose and turned to leave. But she couldn't. She looked back at the shadowy figure behind the grill. "Mother," she floundered. "I'm confused and frightened."

Mother Mary Henriette spoke gently. "Please sit. Tell me why you are frightened."

It was difficult to explain. "On the airplane I sat next to a personable young man. We drank together. We ate. We talked about Don Quixote and Saint Teresa. When I reached the parador here and started to unpack I discovered that I had his bag. It looked much like mine. I was rushing because I thought I might be late for my appointment with you and I picked up the wrong suitcase."

"Your appointment with me?"

"Yes. The sister who met me at the airport said I was to give the box to you at 11:30 yesterday morning. But I was late and that's when Señor Carlos called to explain and he said you were at prayers and I should come this morning."

"I was not expecting you."

"You weren't?"

"No, but go on. You discovered that you had the wrong luggage."

"I went down to buy clothes to wear until we could straighten the whole thing out." She smiled. "But most Spanish women aren't so tall as I and I couldn't find a skirt long enough."

54

She glanced at the pink shirt she had put on this morning and the expensive slacks. "So, I'm still wearing his clothes."

"And I should say they are quite becoming."

"His passport was in his suitcase and he knew where I'd be staying and that I'm going on to Salamanca so I expected to hear from him."

"I am sure you will."

"I'm afraid not. As I was lingering over breakfast, I looked at the front page of the newspaper and it said. . . ." Sydney paused and took a deep breath. "It said he had fallen, or been pushed, from a wall and found dead at the bottom."

"Your personable young man from the airplane?"

"Yes."

"How do you know? How was he identified?"

"By a credit card. His name is Ben Harris and he said he was off to follow one of Don Quixote's adventures. And, he said he's a private investigator."

"Somehow it all sounds a bit contrived." Mother Mary Henriette laughed softly. "But what do I understand of the world? Was he investigating something in Spain?"

"I don't know. He didn't say. At the time it didn't seem to matter. I was more interested in his pursuit of Don Quixote."

"Are you going to Salamanca today?"

"No. I'm staying here until I learn what happened. At least until I can talk with the police. Thank you for listening." Sydney rose. "You said you were not expecting me."

"No. Perhaps the telephones. They are quite unpredictable you know. And we do not have one of those convenient fax machines.

"I will keep the box with the relic. We will find the origin.

Bless you my dear for your merciful mission. Please let me know what you learn of poor Mr. Harris."

Back in the bright sunlight of the courtyard Sydney felt uneasy. In the tiny, cool, dark room, talking with Mother Mary Henriette, she had believed that perhaps it would yet be all right.

She glanced toward the flowerbed beside the gate as she and the nun walked to her car. The man in cowboy boots was gone.

Driving out of the lot she was preoccupied.

Who was Ben Harris really?

Why was he killed? Who killed him?

Was he a PI?

If he was, what was he investigating?

Or, for that matter, was he actually going to write a play about one of Don Quixote's adventures?

Torres watched the Reardon woman follow an old nun into the courtyard. He crossed himself. How could they do anything about diamonds in a monastery? That was Hugo's problem. He was taking care of the cop. The car was parked across the way but no sign of the driver. He moved cautiously toward the corner of the building and peered into an overgrown orchard. No one in sight. He took two steps, the silencer in place, his gun at the ready.

"That's far enough," an invisible voice said in English.

Torres turned.

"Far enough," the voice repeated.

Torres spun and fired toward the sound. There was a groan and he could see a body slump against the trunk of a gnarled tree. He took a careful step. No movement.

"Get up," Torres ordered in English, remembering that the man had spoken English. Probably because his suit was American. It pleased him that all of his suits were made in the United States. "Get up." He approached the figure stretched face down on the ground. With the toe of his shoe he nudged the lump.

A hand suddenly grabbed his ankle and Torres fell on his back, dropping the gun.

The policeman was on top of him plummeting his face. Torres rolled to one side and caught a leg but his hand slipped and came away bloody.

"I hit you."

There was no answer.

The cop still had enough strength to roll Torres over and hold him down while he fastened handcuffs behind his back. Blood was seeping through his pant leg just above the knee.

"Get up."

Torres could see sweat on the man's forehead He was pale and his breathing was labored. He started to get up as ordered and then hesitated, buying time.

"Move." The gun was menacingly close to his face.

"Where?"

"Over there." He pointed to the sedan. "Give me your keys."

Torres considered running but changed his mind. He threw the keys on the ground.

The man in black moaned as he leaned over. With difficulty he reached down and picked up the keys. When he straightened there was a spot of blood on the dirt.

He was moving in slow motion and Torres knew it would not be long but the gun did not waver. He walked to the car.

The policeman unlocked the trunk. "Get in," he ordered as the lid lifted.

"Are you crazy?"

The butt of the gun came down on the side of his head and Torres pitched forward into the trunk.

By leaning against the car to rest several times he managed

to get his belt off and strap Torres' feet. "God," he breathed, "don't let me black out." He hadn't prayed in a long time. "Help me." With the last of his strength he used his handkerchief to gag Torres.

He slammed the trunk lid and then saw blood on the ground. He couldn't clear it all away but with a boot he covered much of it with sand before he fell into the bushes beside the driveway. He mumbled into the mobile and dropped it. The last thing he saw was a big bald head beyond the car.

Hugo Wolf looked around for Torres. There were car keys on the ground. When he picked them up there was blood.

Christ, Torres has got hisself shot.

He had watched Sydney Reardon come out and walk to the car with a nun. They had talked for a minute before she sped away. He should have killed them both but just as he was about to get his bulk through the gate he saw a nun and a priest coming toward him. It was crazy to kill them all if you didn't have to. Besides, she hadn't taken the box into the monastery. Unless it was in her purse.

"Shit," Hugo said aloud.

Leave the Porsche for now. He got into the sedan and drove down the hill.

Peter answered on the first ring just as he had when she called earlier.

"Peter, you answer so quickly. I'm not accustomed to that. It seems everyone either has an answering machine with some message meant to be amusing or there is no response until after many rings."

"Where are you?"

"In Avila still. I'm going to be here for a time. I told you there was a mix-up in luggage. Well, Ben Harris, a young man with whom I became acquainted on the plane, and whose bag I have, fell from the walls here. He's dead."

"Dreadful."

"So, I can't leave until I talk with the police and see what I can learn."

"No, of course not. I'll come down and have dinner with you."

"Dear heart, that's kind but you needn't."

"I'll be there. A little after eight."

"Is Santiago there?"

"Not yet. If he doesn't arrive in time I'll leave a note."

"Of course I'd love to see you but I wish you wouldn't."

"I'll meet you at the parador between eight and half-past."

Sydney was startled when the telephone rang almost as soon as she'd hung up. Peter must have forgotten something. She answered in that breathless way that was her custom. Friends teased her, saying she sounded as if she'd just rushed in and picked up the phone or was leaving and had to run back.

Maude claimed Sydney had answered that way back when they were at school. Maude had all sorts of recollections one couldn't be sure about. "You thought it was dramatic then and it became a habit," she told Sydney.

"Hello." There was no voice on the line. She waited.

"Sydney?"

She did not say yes or no. "Who is this?"

"If I choose I may be all the Twelve Peers of France and the Nine Worthies as well." He chuckled. "Sorry. When I'm nervous I revert to Don Quixote."

"Who *is* this?" she repeated sharply. Was it fear that the voice was familiar or that it wasn't that made her heart skip a beat?

"It's Ben. Ben Harris."

"You're dead."

"Well," he paused. "Or else they were rehearsing in jest what they meant to perform in earnest."

"Stop it. Stop quoting Cervantes. You're alive? Then who was found at the foot of the wall?"

"Wearing your pantyhose? Damned if I know but I suspect everyone is supposed to think I'm dead."

"Where are you?"

"At a public phone near Saint Teresa's church. Bet you didn't know there was a public phone in the neighborhood."

61

"You sound cavalier about death—or murder—or whatever it was."

"Sorry. Oh, I don't have your bag. While I was out they made off with it."

"While you were out? Who made off with it?"

"I'll tell you everything when I see you."

"I have your bag and your clothes."

"And my passport and quite a lot of money I hope."

"Yes luv. What on earth are you doing with fifty thousand dollars in cash?"

"Didn't your mother teach you to never leave home without money? Mine did."

"You are too much. Too, too much. Do you want to come along to the parador so we can compare notes?"

"Not yet. We can talk better here. But we do need to compare notes. Can you meet me? There's a little café on the corner opposite the church. We can have a cup of coffee. You'l recognize me. I'm wearing wrinkled clothes from yesterday."

She could see him flashing the smile. Sydney laughed in spite of herself. "You'll recognize me too. I have on your wonderfu pink shirt."

"Wow. One of my favorites. Glad you like it."

Ben was on his feet as she walked through the door of the tiny café. Hugging her he pulled out a chair. "Wow, I'm glad you're alive."

"I'm glad *you're* alive. Why shouldn't *I* be alive?"

"Here, coffee, good and strong, laced with brandy."

"Let's clear up a few things." Sydney took a sip. "Good! Was all that off to follow in Don Q's footsteps script you read me on the plane for real? Or was it a cover-up for some other role?"

"All of the above."

"What does that mean?"

"I am off to follow in Don Q's footsteps as soon as we untangle this mess. And I am writing a play. But there is more. I had been hanging around the airport checking all the flights to Spain and Portugal, hoping for a break."

"Why Spain and Portugal?"

"That's a likely way to get illegal goods to Macao and, believe it or not, that's still a big market for smugglers."

"Sounds like an adventure story from the 1930s."

"Or 1830s, or earlier. Pick a date. Anyhow, all of a sudden we had a tip that you were carrying stolen diamonds and some emeralds. All we had was a name and flight number. I was following you only I didn't know who you were.

"I told you I'm a PI. What I didn't tell you is that I'm interested only in smuggling. Even if I were not emotionally involved I'd still be fascinated by smuggling. It's so hard to catch the good ones. Think about it. You can get a fairly accurate count of murders because sooner or later bodies of victims are likely to be found. Same goes for bank robbers or burglars or rapists. Mostly they get caught. But, remember, successful smuggling is undetected smuggling. Has been for thousands of years."

"Interesting. I never thought of smuggling in that light. I've always brought firecrackers back from Mexico for kids, just for fun, but that doesn't count. I've never smuggled anything of importance."

"There was the suggestion that once you might have known about an ancient treasure from a Dublin museum when you arranged to have it, as it were, smuggled into the U.S."

"Jesus! How do you know about that? I didn't, as a matter of fact, know it was stolen. Or a treasure. When I cooked up a scheme to transport it I thought it was a joke."

"I believe you."

"Did you know all of this when we were talking and drinking on the flight over?"

"No. We had a tip. Name. Flight number. And that you were carrying about ten million worth of stones."

"Stones?"

"Diamonds, some emeralds. We thought from the name you were a man. That's why I was startled when we introduced ourselves and you said your name was Sydney Reardon. That's all I knew.

"When the tip came I jumped on the flight. I'd had a bag

64

with me hoping for a break so I was ready. I didn't have time to check you out but I knew I could do that from Madrid.

"Then I discovered my bag was gone and you were gone. I went to the customs people and told them I'd lost my passport and bag and I needed to see the police at once. Of course they took me to the police. They know about you in New York and London faxed me a whole sheaf of information."

"If I say I'm stunned you won't be surprised."

"I know you've had three husbands. The first was killed in Vietnam. The second was Elliott Townsend, a big-time theatrical producer who died of a heart attack. The third was run over and killed in Santa Fe."

"I understand their knowing about Pearson and Townie but John was killed long after all the uproar over the little green man in Ireland. Why do the police know about John?"

"Probably once you've been involved in an international crime they keep track of you. Anyhow, they know. I must say it's bad luck to marry you."

When Sydney looked up she was pale.

"Sorry. That was flippant and insensitive."

"It's all right. I've often thought the same thing. It is bad luck to marry me and I was warned."

"You were warned?"

"That's a story for another time. What else do you know?"

"That you were one of London's darlings. You made the columns, first as an actress, and later as a decorator. You were quite something. Seen at all the right parties and clubs and always on the arm of a handsome man."

Sydney smiled. "I'm not the lighthearted party girl I once was. What else?"

"That your limp was not caused by an accident. You are

terrified of heights and one of those handsome men who turned out to be a thief and a murderer pushed you off a London hotel balcony. An awning caught you before you hit the sidewalk." He reached over and touched her hand. "The police believed you. I believe you too."

She shook her head. "Then why are they keeping track of me? It was a nightmare."

"I can imagine. I don't believe you knew you were carrying millions in stolen gems either. I think you were set up."

"I'm not smuggling gems I can assure you."

"What do you think is in that box? Don't you dare say a relic."

She shook her head and smiled, a little wanly. "But I have all the papers. Peter asked me to do it as a favor."

"I must say it was a clever idea. When they were unloading luggage the other night while you sat so long waiting for take-off, they were hoping to find the stones. They did find some heroin. No diamonds though. Who was to know that you were transporting them in such a unique way."

He grinned at her. "But I do know that the bag you checked contained six packages of powdered red chile, two dozen flour tortillas, a couple of pounds of beans, the summer travel section from two newspapers, five St. John's College catalogs, an opera program, and a pair of cowboy boots. It threw the cops completely. Would have puzzled me too if I hadn't learned you were on your way to Salamanca to visit a Santa Fe friend. Sentimental gifts from home no doubt."

"I was in such a hurry, and knew I was going to be late reaching the monastery, so I didn't bother to pick up the suitcase of goodies for Peter. With all that has happened since, I had forgotten about it. I'll have to find it and arrange to have it sent to Salamanca.

"Luv, I need some fresh air." Sydney brushed long fingers across her forehead. "And a little time to take in all of this. And then a stiff drink. Brandy and coffee won't do it."

"Right. Let's sit in the shade of the church for a bit. Then I noticed what looks like a good, dark, smelly bar."

They walked over to the old church.

"Here." Ben swept leaves off a bench. "Where are the stones now?"

"Yesterday I placed your fifty thousand and the box in the safe at the parador. Your cash is still there. I took the box to the monastery this morning."

"Scotch," he said a quarter of an hour later when they were seated in a corner of the bar. "With a splash of water. And bourbon on the rocks." Ben turned to Sydney as the waiter left. "I don't believe this is a place for Black Label." Smiling, he reached over and covered her hands with his. "Can't put this off any longer. Who set you up? Peter?"

"Of course not."

"Then who did?"

"I haven't the faintest idea. You must believe that I was convinced that I was carrying a relic."

"I do believe you. Start at the beginning. Remember. Tell me slowly, carefully, every step that led to your getting the box."

"Peter called. What's today? Sunday? It must have been Monday or Tuesday because I was going to New York on Wednesday to spend a couple of days. Santiago had asked him to ask me if I'd bring the little finger from the left hand of a priest murdered in the 1600s."

"Who's Santiago?"

"Peter's son. His mother was Spanish. A girl Peter met here during the civil war. He didn't know Santiago existed for a long time. In the last few years, and now, particularly since Peter has been teaching in Spain, they're close."

"Where does he live? What does he do?"

"In Madrid. I'm not sure what he does. Works for some large corporation I think. Peter, and perhaps Santiago, will be joining me for dinner tonight. Meet us and you can ask any questions you like."

"Perhaps I will."

"Good. Eightish. At the parador."

"Didn't it seem odd to you that he was asking his father to have you bring a relic?"

"No. Not at all. Peter knows the Carmelites in Santa Fe. Their monastery is just next to St. John's. Since I've lived there I've become interested in them too and support them modestly. Nothing significant. Small checks, champagne, fresh asparagus in early spring. No. It didn't seem odd at all."

"Is it the finger of a Carmelite?"

"I don't think so. The nun who gave it to me said it was a priest martyred in the Pueblo Revolt in 1680 in what is now New Mexico."

"But it was given to you by a Carmelite. And you were instructed to deliver it to a monastery in Carmelite-oriented Avila."

"Yes."

"What were the instructions for you to follow?"

"A sister from a convent on Long Island would meet me at the airport and give me the box. It was simple."

"Where is the convent?"

"I don't know."

"You didn't ask."

"No. Why should I?"

"What was the nun like? Young? Old? What was her name? What did she say?"

"I don't remember her name. Sister Mary something. Their names are so similar. She gave me a box and a sheaf of papers and a letter to Mother Mary Henriette in Avila. Oh, and the biography of Saint Teresa I was reading on the plane."

"Was the book signed?"

"Yes. By the mother superior. It thanked me for the merciful task I was performing and sent best wishes from her and the sisters."

"How do you know it was from the mother superior? What is her name?"

"The nun told me. And, you can read the mother part but I can't make out the rest. I'll show it to you. I remember thinking that with her handwriting she should have been a doctor."

"You haven't told me. What did the sister look like?"

"She was small, wiry, had a deep, husky voice. Wearing a brown habit of course. I don't know, probably in her fifties. Sixties? That's all I know. It's my turn now. Why are you not dead? Jesus, I'm glad you're not, but fill me in."

"What's happened to me relates back to you."

"Back to me?"

"Yes. The minute I pulled the bag down from overhead I knew it wasn't mine. Close but not the right one. So, I had no passport and no money except about fifty dollars stuffed in my pocket. Luckily I had a credit card.

"When I told the Madrid police that I was working with the New York police they said in Spanish the equivalent of, Yeah!?. Finally I persuaded them to call. I had a code the NYPD confirmed and then to make sure they took a mug shot of me and faxed it.

"I finally got them to call here and have someone follow you. All this took a while as you can imagine."

"I was being followed?"

"Yes. I know where you had lunch. By the time I reached the parador you had gone out shopping and I missed you."

"Didn't find anything long enough so I'm still wearing your clothes."

"You look great. As I said, that's one of my favorite shirts.

"I told them I'd watch out for you and they agreed though it seemed to make them nervous. I wouldn't be surprised if they have someone following us both. I decided to go up to your room and see if a little gadget they gave me in school really would open a door. I was going to go in and shower and shave and get clean clothes. When I started to try the lock I heard voices so I walked away. Two men came out. A big bald guy and another who dragged a leg. I followed them to a grove of trees near the wall and slipped from tree to tree trying to hear what they were saying. They climbed up one of the towers. Just as I got near enough to look the big guy pushed the other one over. I was so shocked I shouted and someone started shooting at me. I flattened out on the ground and thought I was gone for sure. Then some kids came along and the bad guys took off. I waited to be certain they were gone and when I stood up I hit my head on a tree limb and knocked myself cold." He displayed the familiar smile. "Some smart PI."

Sydney laughed. "Are you all right now?"

"I think so. There's a knot on top of my head and I have a headache. When I move suddenly I'm dizzy. But, wow, when I first opened my eyes I was like Troy Aikman when he got knocked out and didn't know what he ate for breakfast.

"My car was gone with your bag and my credit card which I'd left on the seat. I'd walk a little way. Or stagger a way. Then I'd

71

have to sit down. I thought I'd stretch out under a tree for a few minutes to try to clear my head and when I moved again it was morning.

"I'm guessing they thought I was a cross-dresser because of your clothes in the car so they put pantyhose on the poor guy who was pushed and left my credit card. I've been talking to the police. They haven't identified the body yet. I could give a pretty good description of the bald guy who did the pushing. He was plenty mean looking. He had a dead cigarette hanging out of his mouth and he had a funny, high-pitched giggle that was completely out of character for a man so big."

"Otro?" the barkeep asked.

Sydney glanced around the dingy room. "I'm ready for sunshine again."

"Right," Ben agreed. "I think I'll shower now and change clothes."

As they strolled toward the parador, Ben continued. "To lead up to what happened yesterday I have to go back a ways. You asked me on the airplane why I was a PI and I passed it off saying in books and films they lead exciting lives. That's not the real reason.

"I had a strange childhood. I lived entirely in a fantasy world. I read a lot. If I had only known Don Q then. I had to be content with Jules Verne and the *Jungle Book* and wild comics. I was frail, as my mother put it. From my father's viewpoint I was a sissy. He was macho in a polished, confident kind of way. He scared me to death. He was fifty-six when I was born. My mother was younger than I am now. She's still somewhat childlike. She's darling looking, lots of fun, but a real space cadet. She loves gambling, especially in Monte Carlo. Her favorite reading is *The Inquirer*. Her favorite recreation is going to fortune tellers."

Sydney cleared her throat and swallowed hard.

"Am I boring you? This does all lead somewhere. I promise."

"No. No. Go on. I'm intrigued."

"Anyhow, my mother was a cocktail waitress in the most fashionable bar in Trinidad, Colorado, if there was a fashionable

73

drinking spot there. My father was in the neighborhood on a shooting trip and stopped for a drink. He fell for her immediately and adored her the rest of his life."

"Your father's dead?"

"Yes. He was killed by a bolt of lightning on a golf course on a day when there was one little cloud in the sky. Can you believe that? I was eleven."

"Yes. I can believe most anything since I was tossed over a balcony by my best friend and my husband was run over and killed when he walked out to get the Sunday paper."

"I know, sometimes it doesn't all make sense."

He mouths a platitude carelessly, Sydney thought, as the young often do. As I probably did when I was older than he.

"As you've guessed, my father had lots of money so Betsy was set up and so am I. To be perfectly candid, I was somewhat relieved to be out of his shadow. If I may lift another line from Don Q, '. . . the thought of a legacy possesses the magic power to remove, or at least to soothe the pangs that the heir would otherwise feel. . . .'"

"Family money, or was he self-made?"

"Oh, he made it himself. Do you know what happened in 1950?"

"Hm," Sydney pondered. "G. B. Shaw, Edna St. Vincent Millay and Al Jolson died. The two hundredth anniversary of Bach's death was celebrated and Ohio State won the Rose Bowl."

"Wow! How can you remember all those things?"

"I don't know. I sometimes have trouble with important information but I can recall all sorts of trivia. Don't say it, I should have been on one of those television shows."

Ben laughed. "Well for my family something else significant happened. Antihistamines became a popular remedy for colds

74

and allergies. My father was a pharmaceutical salesman and a bright, ambitious, aggressive guy. He found some investors and they made a ton of money in the legal drug market.

"So Betsy never has to want for anything. And, bless her, neither do I."

"Pretty interesting story but what does all this have to do with being a PI?"

"I'm coming to that. My father had an older sister, my Aunt Daphne. She never married. She lived in an apartment near us which, looking back, I'm sure was paid for by my father. I used to spend a good bit of time there. She was wonderful, a little fey but kind and patient and amusing.

"Her proudest possession was my grandmother's diamond ring. Not so large but an unusual perfect triangular cut. She had read about diamonds and was especially intrigued by one a diamond trader named Tavernier brought to Paris where it was sold to Louis XIV. It was cut into a triangular stone weighing some sixty-eight carats. It was stolen in 1792 and never recovered. About forty years later the diamond now known as the Hope appeared on the market. It was probably part of the larger missing stone.

"Anyhow, her love of diamonds intrigued family members and over time they gave, or left, her several.

"She spent her last years in a nursing facility. I went to see her often. She was a bit vague about the present but still entertaining with stories about growing up and about her little brother, my father.

"She kept her cache of diamonds in a chamois pouch that she stuffed down the front of her dress to safety in her saggy bosom. It delighted her to spread the seven or eight stones out on a little table beside her chair and tell about each one and then carefully return them to their safe place.

"Guess what? When she died and we went to collect her things, the diamonds were gone."

"No!"

"I was angry. I couldn't get anywhere with the police. They weren't listening. I kept asking questions and digging and trying to find out what happened and I became convinced there is a ring that steals jewelry from old folks in nursing homes. They use sympathetic attendants who move around to places in affluent neighborhoods. As you can imagine, the turnover is high. So, it's been hard to track them.

"I made up my mind to break the ring for Aunt Daphne so I went to PI school. Since I finished I've been on the case. Once the police decided I was not some kind of nut and they knew I didn't want to be paid they've let me work on it. You wondered why I was carrying so much money. I don't know if I could kill anyone so I thought it might work to use bribery."

He grinned at her. "Although I really am a licensed investigator, this is my first case. Make you nervous?"

"No," she assured without hesitation as she smiled. "This is the first time I've smuggled millions of dollars worth of stones as you call them. So, we're even. What do we do next?"

"We go to your room and I clean up. I'll slip up the back stairs."

Sydney went through the lobby, checking for messages at the desk. It was a habit she'd had since early theatre days when messages could be *so* important. Nothing. As she unlocked her door she saw Ben moving along the corridor.

"She gasped. "Jesus! Ben!"

His footsteps were loud in the empty hallway as he ran toward her room. He stopped behind her in the doorway. "Oh, my god!"

76

The bed had been torn apart. Every drawer from the chest by the window was in the middle of the floor. His clothes were strewn around the room.

"Where's the box? Did they get it?"

"No. I gave it to Mother Mary Henriette."

"By now they've figured that. Come on. Let's go."

Sydney ignored the pain of running as she followed him down the stairs to the car park.

"You drive," Ben ordered. "You know the way. Fast."

"I can't drive fast in these streets."

"Yes you can. Put your foot to the floor."

"And shut my eyes."

Ben Harris didn't laugh. He hadn't even heard her.

Sydney backed out of the parking area, headed through the gate and pressed her foot to the floor. She was a skillful driver but she surprised herself by the daring and speed with which she avoided pedestrians and maneuvered through narrow streets. She loved driving fast but this was a new experience.

"Jesus, even if I don't kill someone the police are going to pick us up."

"Pray that the police notice us," Ben muttered. "Look,"

he pointed. "That's the car I followed from the parador to the wall where the murder took place."

He reached in his pocket and pulled out a tiny gun.

"Is that a toy?"

"I hope not. It's a hideout handgun. I carry it in my pocket with just a handkerchief around it to mask the outline and nobody knows. I'm so slim, anything bigger and I'd have to wear a coat all the time to conceal it."

"You said you weren't sure you could shoot anybody. Is it really effective?"

"Not bad at close range. Let's hope I don't have to find out. There's the Porsche. I don't like this. Find a phone and call the police."

"I can't leave you here alone."

"You must. Hurry."

Sydney watched him rushing toward the monastery. Should she follow, or go for help? Emotionally she leaned toward the first option but common sense told her it was wiser to call the police.

Ben's heart was pounding as he approached the formidable stone building. The first challenge would be getting inside those walls.

Unfortunately it was possible. The great wooden gate that must have protected the order for centuries hung at an awkward angle, the hinges cut out in a crazy pattern by gunfire. It looked as if a child's wooden toy had been sawed from around the ancient iron straps.

He pushed the heavy door. Even wounded it did not yield easily. Finally, leaning with all his strength, he pushed a bottom corner far enough to squeeze through.

He saw no one. There was not a sound. Staying close to the vine-covered walls, he moved slowly toward the long porch that outlined the cloister. In the center of the courtyard was a well. Flowers bloomed in a circular bed surrounding it. Suddenly the vines beside him rustled. He swung around and stiff-armed, leveled the small gun. A bird, as startled as he, fluttered to freedom in the yard.

Step by step he continued, moving closer to the protection of the porch. Just ahead there was a path. If he followed it he would be an easy target for anyone against the vines. Stay near the edge, beside the wall, he warned himself.

There was a door in the long wall. He knocked gently at first and then harder. "Hello." In the stillness he felt he was shouting. "Hello. Anyone there?"

No response.

Slowly, quietly. Watch for any movement. Listen for the slightest sound, he cautioned himself. Take it easy. This is a bad scene.

There was a door in the tall façade ahead. He had to cross a few yards of open ground. Quickly. Not a sound except his footsteps. Just in front of the door there was something on the stone floor. Inching forward he leaned down to look.

"No, no, no," he whispered. The front of the brown habit was covered with blood. Ben knelt beside the body. "Wow," he murmured reverently. She had been shot head-on.

"No se mueva."

He didn't look around. He didn't understand Spanish but he knew he'd been ordered not to move.

Did he drop the gun or did the man in uniform push it away? He'd never remember for sure.

"Parate, lentamente. Con cuidado."

It was clear from the motions and the tone of voice that he was being told to stand up slowly and not make a false move.

The officer in charge motioned to another policeman to cover him while he walked to the door Ben had been moving toward when he discovered the body.

The man was knocking softly but with authority.

"Policía. Está bien. Por favor, abran la puerta."

Police he could figure out. Whatever else the officer said must have been reassuring for a smaller door opened from the lower section of the tall door and a brown-clad figure emerged.

Removing his hat, the officer spoke quietly to the sister. She started forward. He restrained her while a policeman took off his coat and covered the lifeless figure on the stone floor.

He motioned to the man who was watching Ben and they herded him after the nun into a small, dimly lit room.

Ben was startled when he heard a voice from the corner. Looking around he could see a shadowy figure behind a grill.

"Capitan, qué pasó? Hubo voces irritadas en el paseo. Hubo tiros de escopeta y luego silencio."

"Madre Maria Henrietta." The captain paused and took a deep breath. *"Temo que han matado a la Hermana Teresa Eloisa."*

He couldn't follow the conversation but he caught Mother Mary Henriette. The one Sydney had mentioned.

"Excuse me. You're Mother Mary Henriette. I'm Ben Harris."

"But you are dead," she said easily in English.

Almost the exact words Sydney had used when he called her.

"You know this man Mother?" the captain asked in careful English.

"We have not met but I know who he is. He is a friend of Sydney Reardon who delivered a box yesterday. She said it contained a relic but I fear that was not the case."

80

"Sydney thought so," Ben said quickly.

"I know she did," the mother superior agreed.

It took a while to explain the situation to Captain Marquez. When he couldn't quite follow Ben's English, Mother Mary Henriette helped out.

"Where is Sydney Reardon now?"

"Didn't she call you to come here?"

"No. We had a call from an officer who was at the monastery. He's been shot but will recover."

"That's bad. When I came in here I sent Sydney to call for help. That was . . . ?" He looked at his watch. "Seems like hours. Half an hour ago."

"Please excuse me. I must send Sister María Rosa to tell the parents of Sister Teresa Eloisa of the tragedy. And, after this blasphemous act we must plan for having the monastery reconsecrated."

"Sister Teresa Eloisa grew up in Avila," Captain Marquez explained as the mother superior left. "She went to school with my daughter. She was carefree and a little wild. Bright. She was a leader. I will have to go to her parents. What will I say?" He shook his head. "I am sorry. That will not comfort them."

"Come. I will give you a ride. There are still questions."

They walked back into the late afternoon sunshine. Ben tried to put aside the horror he had just witnessed and focus on a question. Where is Sydney?

Sydney flew down the narrow path leading away from the monastery. Where was the nearest telephone?

As she was rounding a turn at the bottom of the hill a man stumbled from the bushes directly in front of her car. She braked hard and came to a stop as he rolled to the side.

While she was catching her breath and looking to be sure the one who had fallen was all right, the passenger door opened and a great hulk of a man climbed in.

"Who are you?"

He pulled out a long-barreled, old-fashioned gun and pointed it her way.

Sydney shivered. The plenty-mean-looking bald guy Ben had described was in the seat beside her.

"Maybe a friend. Maybe not. We'll see."

The man who had been on the ground in front of the car appeared at the window on her side.

"Take this car and lose it," the man beside Sydney ordered. He motioned for her to get out and into a sedan that had pulled up behind them. "You drive."

She could feel her knees shaking as she eased the car forward. "Where?"

"Out the road to Salamanca. Know the way?"

Sydney nodded, not trusting her voice.

"Stop here."

She pulled off the highway in the exact spot where she had planned to pause for a look at the walled city behind her.

The man placed the barrel of the gun close to her cheek. "Give me the keys. Get out. Slow." He climbed out after her and pointed back toward Avila. "Pretty from here, huh?" He used his thumbnail to strike a match, lighted a cigarette and flipped the match away.

Suddenly Sydney was more angry than frightened. Her knees were wobbly and she knew her hands were shaking but her voice was strong. "You didn't bring me here for the view. We both know that."

"We're just killin' a little time if you'll pardon my sayin' it that way." He giggled. "Waiting for the light to fade. You're noticeable walkin' around now. You're not raving about the view. Guess you've seen it before."

"Yes. Several times."

"You good friends with the nuns? That why you ran there?"

"I don't know them at all. I've never been to the convent."

"You're lyin'. You went there this morning. Why?"

"I'm not lying. I mean I've never been to the convent before this morning."

"Why did you go today?"

"To give a message to Mother Mary Henriette."

"You mean to give her a box."

"No."

"That's what the nun said. You didn't give them a box. I think she was lyin' too. She kept sayin' that and comin' forward. She said that right up until I shot her."

83

"You shot a nun!"

He nodded. "Had to. She wasn't scared of nothin'."

Sydney put a hand over her mouth.

He shook his head slowly. "We tore the place apart and didn't find it."

"You tore my room apart earlier this afternoon and didn't find anything there either. Just not your lucky day."

"Don't smart ass me." Taking a step forward he clutched the weapon in frustration. He was no taller than Sydney but his bulk was menacing. She stepped back. "What happened at your place was nothing. I wish you'd of seen that convent and that nun and you'd know by Christ I mean business. Only had to kill one. She was feisty. I'll give her that. I told her to stop twice but she wouldn't."

Suddenly a bullet whizzed past Sydney's shoulder. She spun around as a rabbit flopped into the air, gave a short squeal and fell dead.

Hugo Wolf giggled.

Sydney steadied herself against the car. "What was that?"

"What?"

"I heard a sound. A thump."

"Probably your heart."

"Listen, comedian, I'm certain I heard a sound behind the car."

"I'd say you're just tryin' to get me to look away." He stepped back, careful to keep the gun trained on Sydney. He stood behind the car, listening. With his left hand he took keys from his pocket and opened the trunk.

"Shit, Torres how'd you get there?"

Sydney took a step to try to look into the trunk.

"Stay right there. Don't take one more step."

84

The man reached into the trunk and tugged at an obviously heavy object. After two or three jerks he pulled a gagged, handcuffed man from the trunk and let him drop to the ground.

Sydney gasped.

Hugo yanked the gag from the man's mouth.

"Who stuffed you in there? That cop with the boots?"

"Yes," the man on the ground whispered hoarsely.

"Is the cop dead?"

"I think so."

"You *think* so!"

"I shot him but he still got me. He was bleeding so much I'm sure he's dead. Water. Please."

"Maybe he's not. You told me you're careful and intelligent. You ain't either."

Sydney started when the revolver went off. "Jesus, does it amuse you to shoot a man just like it does to shoot a rabbit?"

"'Bout the same." He motioned toward the car. "Get in. Light's right now for us to move."

"You can't just leave that man."

"He's dead. Get in. We're going to the parador."

"The parador?"

"Yeah. Go."

After what she had just witnessed Sydney decided her chance of survival was infinitesimal. She drove as slowly as she dared. Not a police car in sight. Hardly any cars on the road at this hour with siesta over and shops still open.

She pulled into the almost empty car park.

"Leave the keys in and get out."

He was following closely behind her. "The back stairs."

Before they reached the door the man who had stumbled in front of her emerged from the bushes and drove the car away.

85

A couple walked toward them along the corridor. The big man dropped behind her with the gun close to his thigh on the wall side.

Sydney smiled stiffly at the man and woman as they passed. She considered attracting their attention but thought better of it. She would be dead. They would probably be dead too.

"Here." He stopped, reaching to unlock the door.

"The room next to mine?"

"We thought it would be . . ." The giggle again. ". . . convenient."

The Avila police asked surprisingly few questions. Did they believe him, Ben wondered, or were they convinced he was not leaving town?

The room was a mess. Why didn't he call for a maid to straighten it? Almost superstitious. Sydney was superstitious she said. Perhaps he was too. He had to right the room himself. He folded his clothes carefully, placing them, almost mechanically, in the drawers he had returned to their runners.

He kept looking at his watch. Soon he could meet Peter Farber. Without Sydney it was not going to be easy.

Ben positioned himself near the entrance and ordered bourbon.

The old man paused in the doorway of the bar and looked around. It had to be Peter. Sydney said he seemed a little unsteady on his long legs as if he were walking on stilts.

Ben stood and moved toward him. "You must be Peter Farber."

He was looking down on Ben with a puzzled expression.

"I'm Ben Harris. Sydney has told me about you."

"You're dead," the man said in a deep, quiet voice.

Ben laughed uneasily. "Well, I'm not, but I expect I'm supposed to be."

"Where's Sydney?"

"I'll explain. Over here. Please." He pulled out the other chair.

"Where's Sydney?"

She had told him that Peter didn't waste words. He was so direct that this was even harder than he had anticipated. "I don't know." Ben took a deep breath. "She's disappeared."

"When? Where? Have you called the police? She told me you're enamored of Don Quixote. Don't be quixotic now."

"This afternoon. After she left me at the convent. Yes, I've talked with the police."

"Why aren't you dead?"

"It's a real fluke. I was following two guys I saw come out of Sydney's room and one of them pushed the other one off a wall. It shocked me and I shouted and a couple of henchmen started shooting at me. I hit the ground thinking I was finished for sure. Then a bunch of kids came along and they took off. I waited until I was sure the cars had driven away and when I stood up I hit my head on a tree limb and knocked myself out cold."

Peter Farber was looking at him as if he were an idiot. "And?"

"By the time I regained consciousness they were gone and so was my car and my credit card and Sydney's bag which was in the car."

Peter didn't say anything, just continued staring at him.

"I'm guessing when they found women's clothes in the car they figured I was a cross-dresser and that's why the poor guy at the foot of the wall was wearing pantyhose. And he was identified by my credit card on the body."

"You'd better do some explaining."

The waiter returned with Peter's Scotch and water and he took a good swallow, watching Ben and waiting.

"Yes. You tell me what you know about Sydney that may be helpful and I'll tell you all I know, or can piece together. For starters, how do you know Sydney and for how long?"

"Her," Peter sighed, "late husband was my best friend. He was an anthropologist and art historian. Good combination. We met at The Palace in Santa Fe. It was a busy noontime and we were both having a sandwich at the bar. I don't usually make conversation. I'm a loner."

Just what Sydney told me, Ben thought.

"His home base was Santa Fe but he worked mostly in Mexico and Central America. He had just come back from looking at some rock art in Baja and he talked about light and time and space. I had seen those magnificent pictures on rocks but I didn't read all that into them. I was fascinated.

"We became friends and I went with him on a few trips. Then he was on a big project in Oaxaca and when he came back he called me to meet him at The Palace for a drink on Friday. That's not a good time because it's lecture night at St. John's and neither tutors nor students make a habit of missing lectures.

"Well, I did. John was all fired up. He'd met this woman in a bar in Oaxaca and he was mad about her. It was a whirlwind thing and he said it was mutual. She had come back with him to Santa Fe.

"'Be careful, John,' I cautioned, remembering some of the women I'd met in bars. He assured me she was beautiful, light-hearted, wonderful. I was still not convinced. She sounded too good to be true.

"He insisted that I had to get to know her and invited me

to join them for dinner on Wednesday which was my birthday. I agreed. I was busy with my seminar on Monday night and a preceptorial on Tuesday and I didn't give it a thought until I looked at my calendar and saw it was Wednesday. A freshman came by in late afternoon. He was about to give up and I spent more time than I expected with him so I was late reaching the restaurant.

"I stopped in the doorway and was looking around for them. Just as I spotted them Lino, the owner, came over and led me to their booth.

"She hadn't noticed me. She was attentive to something John was telling her. All I could see was her cheek and shiny dark hair. Then John must have told her I was there and she turned toward me with a brilliant smile.

"John stood up to introduce us. Sydney stood. She surprised me by giving me a big hug and I surprised myself by hugging her back.

"The first thing I knew we were all talking, drinking, laughing, and it was a delight. When Sydney's with you she's genuinely glad to be there." He was smiling for the first time since they met. "I sometimes suspect she may not give you a thought when she's not with you but you feel great in her company."

The old boy's in love with Sydney, Ben thought, and liked him a lot. I'm a little in love with her too. She's too young for him and too old for me but it sure is fun to dream about what if.

They were already finishing their second drinks. "Let's order another round," Ben suggested. "And some food."

Peter recommended the paella and Ben went along, not really caring what he ate.

"How long have you known Sydney?"

"About three years. She and John were married almost two years and he's been gone a year now."

"Must have been a terrible shock."

"It was, because they were perfect for one another. Also, she felt guilty because she'd been warned."

"She mentioned that. When I questioned her she backed off."

"Her mother took her and a couple of friends to a fortune teller for her birthday when Sydney was eleven or twelve and the woman told the other girls the usual about good grades and marrying rich, handsome men. After looking at Sydney's palm she warned her that she should be careful about marrying—she'd outlive her husbands."

"Strange thing to tell a child."

"Yes. I think Sydney probably didn't give it much thought until she was in college and went to a fortune teller again. Looking back she wonders why. That one told her she'd be married three times and outlive all her husbands. When she met John she told him and, of course, he laughed. But the prophecy came true."

"The first one was killed in Vietnam and the second one died of a heart attack."

"How do you know this? I can't imagine Sydney telling you all that on an overnight airplane ride."

Scotch is a wonder, Ben mused. He's becoming more and more talkative.

"No, she didn't. We had a tip that a Sydney Reardon was transporting stolen diamonds. When I checked with the New York and London police I learned a whole lot about her."

"About that messy museum theft in Ireland no doubt and what she refers to as her 'accident' in London."

"Right. Did you know the box contained stolen gems?"

91

"Certainly not." He was no longer feeling the alcohol. No longer hungry either. He pushed the paella aside. "What's this nonsense about stolen gems and tips and Sydney? Who are you?"

Ben was positive that PI was not the right term to use here. "I'm a private investigator. I've been working with the New York police trying to crack a clever ring that steals jewelry from people in nursing facilities. Millions of dollars worth of diamonds and emeralds over the past few years. For the latest shipment we had a name and a flight number.

"This group is bad. Major bad. They killed a guy yesterday who was supposed to be me. They've killed a nun and torn the convent apart. Now they've got Sydney. What do you know about all this? Help me. Help Sydney."

"I don't know anything about stolen diamonds. I asked her to bring a relic and she said yes. I'm sure she didn't give it a thought. I didn't. My god, I didn't know there was anything untoward. I didn't know she'd be in danger or that anyone would be killed."

"Who asked you to persuade Sydney to bring the box?"

"Santiago, my son."

"Did he know all about the relic?"

"I don't know. I think not. He was doing it for a friend in his company."

"What company?"

"La Joya, Ltd. An import firm in Madrid."

"What do they import?"

"They're brokers for American firms doing business in Spain."

"Why didn't Santiago come down to Avila with you tonight?"

He had told the boy as they were getting acquainted over

a first drink, about Santiago's passion for fast cars, about his new Porsche. Ben liked fast cars too so he'd shown him a picture of Santiago's prized toy. He had explained about his son's shooting accident and his game leg and he never did that. Now the fellow wanted to know why Santiago had not come with him to Avila.

"I left before he arrived," Peter Farber said irritably. "Why are you so interested in my son?"

During the conversation Ben's heart had dropped to his shoes. He was pretty certain he knew whose body had been found at the bottom of the wall wearing pantyhose and carrying his credit card.

"Don't go back to Salamanca tonight. We may get some word."

About Sydney, he hoped. Almost surely before too long about Santiago. It was a matter of time before the police identified the body and he didn't want Peter to be alone when he heard.

"There are two beds in Sydney's room. We can camp out there and wait for a call."

"Should go home." Peter sighed. "I'm tired. And a little drunk. I left Santiago a note. Let's call it a night." He passed a big hand across his eyes and leaned on the table as he rose. Ben knew better than to offer a hand.

There were two men climbing the stairs ahead of them. Captain Marquez turned when he heard footsteps.

"There you are. We were just going to check Mrs. Reardon's room."

"This is Sydney's friend Peter Farber. He came down from Salamanca for dinner."

The men shook hands. "Ben has persuaded me to stay over in case there's word from Sydney."

"I'll have someone outside the door. We will wish to question Mrs. Reardon. As soon as she reappears."

"You don't think she's going to reappear," Ben said. "You think we may be . . ." He stopped. "In danger too," he added lamely.

Captain Marquez shrugged.

"Sit there." Hugo pointed to a chair beside a small table in the center of the room. "Easy to watch you there in the middle."

"Obviously you were planning to bring me here. Everything was set beforehand."

"Yeah. I always plan ahead. We don't need a lot of talk. Just tell me where the box is."

"I don't have it."

"That's not what I asked you." He placed both fat hands on the table, leaning forward menacingly. "That's not what I asked you," he repeated. "Where is it?"

Sydney did not answer as she looked up at the big, bald man towering over her.

He drew back one huge paw as if to strike her and then let his arm drop. "Where is it?" he repeated in a voice frighteningly quiet.

Sydney considered her answer. "I don't have it," she said once again.

"Aren't you scared?"

"Of course. But I've been frightened before. You can get only so scared, as you put it. Beyond that you can act, though not always rationally. I'm reaching that point and that's when it becomes dangerous for you."

"I don't know what you're talkin' about. Beautiful watch. I'll take it."

He reached for her wrist.

Sydney jerked back. "No. Let me."

"And those pearls and chains. Rings too."

Sydney removed the jewelry and handed it to him.

"You're not only a murderer, you're a common thief."

"You're smart assin' me again. Be careful. I'll . . ."

Suddenly there was a sound and the bathroom door opened. Hugo spun around.

"Howdy Hugo."

A small, grey, wizened figure entered the room.

"Christ Edna, what are you doin' here?"

Until he called the person by name Sydney had not been sure whether this stranger was a man or a woman.

"Hugo, I wish you wouldn't take the name of our Savior in vain. Andy and Henry picked up that awful habit from you."

"Shit, Edna, you don't make sense. You pay me to kill. You lie. You steal from sick old ladies and you worry about me takin' the name of the Lord in vain? Why are you here?"

"I followed you Hugo. You killed both my boys. I been thinkin' all the way over about what to do with you."

"I only killed Henry," Wolf blurted out. "I had to before he told them everything."

Edna was chuckling—more a gurgle than a laugh.

"That a confession Hugo? You are dumb. Mean and strong but dumb. Henry told them plenty. Andy killed hisself when the police started closin' in. I figure that's the same as you killin' him."

96

"Edna, you blame me for everthing that happens."

"No matter. While the police was foolin' with Andy I cleared out the back door. Where's the box?"

"I wish I knew."

"What've you been doin' since you got here?"

"Followin' her mostly." He nodded toward Sydney. "Santiago fucked up. Had to kill him."

"No great loss. Where's the box?"

"I don't know."

"I bet she does."

She stared at Sydney across the table.

Sydney stared back. This strange creature was somehow familiar. She could be anywhere between fifty and seventy. She could be a man or a woman. She was wearing faded jeans, a blue cotton sweater, a black leather cap, and heavy high-topped shoes. The eyes that peered out from under the bill of the cap were cold and blank. Sydney tried to look away from the evil gaze.

"Don't move," Hugo said.

"Won't she tell you?"

"Ain't really asked her serious yet." He moved the dead cigarette from one corner of his mouth to the other. "I thought it was at the monastery but they said no even after I shot that nun."

"Shot a nun! I should kill you Hugo."

"Unless I kill you first." Hugo started to raise the gun he had been holding by his thigh.

"I wouldn't if I was you."

She nodded and for the first time Hugo realized there was someone else in the room.

"This is my new boy. I named him Hugo."

Named him! Sydney trembled. It was as if the woman were referring to a precocious animal.

"Can you beat that?" Edna was making the gurgling sound that passed for a laugh. "He's a Mesican. Don't speak English but he'll learn. Oh, a few words. He knows 'hit' and 'kick' and 'shoot' and 'kill.' I can't speak Spanish but we communicate. He'll do anything for money. Anything!"

The new Hugo was sauntering toward the old Hugo. He was what—maybe twenty—short and thick with slick black hair. Strong muscles bulged where the white T-shirt sleeves had been cut away. A tattoo of the Virgin of Guadalupe decorated his left forearm. An unfriendly grin revealed two rows of small pointed teeth. He took a step or two, clenching his fists.

"Stop," Edna said and held up a hand as if gesturing to restrain a bright guard dog. He stopped.

Edna gurgled. "Lucky for you that's one of his words. I figured all the way over here what to do about you after I got the box. And now you don't have it."

"We'll get it."

"Maybe. But I bet the police get it first." With her new Hugo beside her, Edna could move at will. She stalked over to fat Hugo reaching up for the dead cigarette in his mouth. She pulled a match from her pocket and struck it on the leg of her jeans. Taking a drag, she blew smoke in the big man's face. "I could of used that ten million Hugo. Sure could of. But I've got a new territory in mind that'll make what we've got so far look puny."

"Then you'll need me Edna."

"Don't think so. I got him. I always know when it's best to do nothin'. That's what I've decided to do about you. Nothin'. Just walk out of here and leave you."

"You can't do that Edna."

"Watch me."

98

The young Hugo put his hand on his hip near the gun in the belt of his jeans and followed Edna out into the hall.

"She can't do that to me," Hugo muttered as the door closed.

Sydney smiled her wide, enchanting smile. "I think she just did."

The blow from his beefy hand knocked her to the floor. She thought her jaw was broken. At any rate it was paralyzed.

"Get up."

Sydney moaned as she tried to rise.

"And shut up."

"Wha," Ben Harris mouthed as he struggled to awaken from a troubled sleep.

He tried again and realized his mouth was covered by a firm hand. Another was placed squarely on his chest. Opening his eyes he saw Peter Farber leaning over him.

"Quiet," Farber whispered.

"Wow. You're strong," Ben said in a low voice as he tried to sit up.

The old man smiled. "I was once." He motioned for Ben to follow as he led the way to the bathroom and pulled the door closed soundlessly.

"Sydney is in the room next door."

"What!"

"Shh."

"How do you know?"

"I couldn't sleep. I was sitting on the balcony. I heard loud voices. And then I heard that voice, unmistakably Sydney's."

"She can't be next door. That's crazy."

"She is. I am certain."

"What do we do?"

"The police captain said they are watching. We go into the hall and tell them."

Remarkable, Ben thought. Peter is taking charge. He was glad to be following the tall, ancient man toward the door.

Farber paused. "Don't shut the door," he whispered. "If I could hear Sydney they can hear us. There must not be a sound."

Captain Marquez was just taking leave of the officers he had assigned to stand guard.

Farber held a long, bony finger to his lips. He motioned Captain Marquez to follow him.

The police officer hesitated and then walked with him down the corridor. Ben trailed.

"Sydney is in the room next to us."

"Impossible Professor."

"I am inclined to agree with you but I heard her."

Marquez quickly walked to the end of the wide hall, paused, and stood with his back to them. Striding back to Peter and Ben he motioned them to remain silent. Again he paced to the end of the corridor, hesitated, and returned.

"If you are correct. . . ." He pointed a finger at Farber. Did he almost smile? "And I believe that you are correct. Surprise is the only thing in our favor. We break the door."

Responding to his motions, two officers moved into position, and stiff-armed, pointed guns toward the door. What kind? Too bad I flunked Guns 101, Ben thought grimly. They looked efficient. He heard soft footsteps and turned. The giant wearing sneakers and carrying an axe looked *really* efficient. Without anyone noticing, Ben dropped behind. He held his breath as the titan struck the door and pushed it open as it quivered.

"Drop it," Marquez ordered in a commanding voice.

Hugo didn't drop the revolver but hesitated for an instant to consider.

"Let us talk."

"Yeah. Let's talk. While we do, you stay there. I'll stay here. She'll stay right there."

"I demand that Mrs. Reardon be allowed to leave the room immediately."

"Why? What's in it for me?"

"What's in it for you?" Marquez said disdainfully. "Your life."

Hugo stood motionless, trying to analyze his options. Suddenly there was a slight sound at the window. He turned his big body to face the interruption.

"Drop it," Marquez said in a cold, quiet voice.

Wolf started to take aim but at that moment a thick rope of gelatinous material hit his hand. He yelled, raised his arm and tried to move away as ooze belched from an odd-looking weapon Ben Harris was pointing at him. As he writhed, rubberous ropes continued to wrap around him like snakes until he was completely immobilized.

"What's that?" Sydney laughed shakily.

"It's a goo gun," Ben explained as he continued to package Hugo in the tenacious material. "It's not lethal but it sure is immobilizing. They perfected it in a lab out near you—in Albuquerque. It's been used in several hot spots around the world. I was thrilled they let me test it because I don't think I can really shoot anybody."

Peter walked over and encircled Sydney with his long arms.

"You're going to the hospital."

Before she could protest, Marquez nodded. "Yes."

Peter stroked her hair. "Overnight. They can check out what is left of your beautiful face. You can get some rest."

Marquez nodded again. "One question. Have you learned anything from this man that may be helpful to us?"

"He's not the one you really want. He takes orders from Edna."

"Edna?"

"She's the brains behind the entire operation. She has a new thug, bodyguard, with her."

With a comforting arm around Sydney's shoulders Farber guided her toward the door.

"Take one of my men to help you and get that mess off," Marquez directed Ben. "I have never seen anything like it." With a hint of a grin he added, "How do you get it off?"

"Baby oil. Salad oil. Any kind of oil I guess." Ben chuckled. "But it will take a while."

Sydney turned back as she was leaving the room. "When you un-goo Hugo you'll find a good bit of my favorite jewelry in his pockets."

Captain Marquez led the way into the old stone building that served as a morgue.

Hugo Wolf was moving reluctantly, herded by a policeman.

Farber lumbered along with his peculiar gait.

Ben Harris followed apprehensively. The only other time he'd been in a morgue was when his PI class visited one in Washington. It had been embarrassing when he felt faint and had to sit while an attendant held a damp cloth to his forehead. Before the thick door opened he could smell what they had told him was embalming material. He was beginning to feel lightheaded.

"Thank you for meeting us here at this hour Doctor," Marquez said in his studied English.

"*De nada*. Over here." The doctor removed a sheet from the body on the table as Marquez pushed Hugo forward.

"In spite of the damage from the fall you can see there is a—how do you call it—a birthmark. Just here."

Shifting uneasily Hugo moved the dangling cigarette from one side of his mouth to the other.

Marquez turned the body to reveal an unusual blemish on one shoulder. As he stepped aside to afford a clear view the corpse flopped heavily to the edge of the slab.

104

A hoarse groan came from deep in Hugo Wolf's throat. "Son-of-a-bitch. You ain't dead." With a lunge he grabbed the body and pushed it to the floor. "Die!" he screamed as he kicked the lifeless object.

"Stop," Marquez ordered as two officers grabbed for Wolf.

One of Hugo's great fists caught the first man square on the jaw. With a moan he fell back under the table and lay still. The second officer made a jump out of the way but Hugo reached out and grabbed him and he sprawled on the concrete floor.

"Stop," Marquez repeated in a calm, careful voice, drawing his service piece from its holster. Hugo took two angry steps toward the captain.

The gunshot was deafening in the cold room.

For an instant Wolf looked startled. Then he collapsed. The dead cigarette that had fallen from his lips lay on the floor near his outstretched hand.

"That little chicken shit had a dream," he whispered. "To kill me. Christ, he did it." The big head rolled to one side.

"We still have no identification," Marquez said tonelessly.

"I can identify the body. Positively." Peter Farber had not moved since he had come into the room and stopped near the head of the table.

Ben leaned against the wall to steady himself.

The police captain was startled by the voice and turned toward Farber.

"He is my son."

"I am sorry. Did you know when I brought you here?"

"No."

Marquez turned to Ben. "Did you know?"

"I suspected when Peter and I were talking. Everything pointed to it—the Porsche, the limp. But I couldn't say anything because I wasn't sure." Ben shrugged, looking at Peter. "Even if I'd been sure I don't think I could have told you."

"Come, let us go to the station. I must ask questions." Marquez looked at Farber. "It is late. Shall we wait until morning?"

"No. We shall go now."

Ben sat in the small, stuffy, poorly lighted waiting room while the two men talked. The news about Santiago would be one more shock for Sydney. At least, thank God, she was safe in the hospital.

"I wish you would stay the rest of the night," Captain Marquez was saying as he came out of his office with Peter.

Farber shook his head.

Ben followed them to the car. "Don't go. Please," he urged. "Stay here."

"I must go. I have to sort it all out." He held out a strong, bony hand and the boy took it. He rather liked Ben Harris. "Look after Sydney. Tell her she'll hear from me."

Ben nodded, closed the car door after him and waved slowly as the old man drove away.

Peter maneuvered easily through the familiar streets. At this hour there was almost no traffic.

He had never left Avila without stopping to look back. He drove into the turn-around as usual, not stopping but circling and enjoying for a moment the glow of lights above the walls.

Santiago is dead. Worse than that he must have been a hired killer. How he loved that boy. Man. He still thought of him as a boy and felt responsible.

"Think of something. Anything rather than Santiago," he said aloud.

What episode among Don Quixote's many adventures was the boy planning to turn into a play?

Anything involving Dulcinea would be too obvious.

It is so wonderfully wordy. Hard to see it on stage. But then *Man of La Mancha* had been a success.

Which episode would I choose if I were writing a play?

The prize of Mambrino's helmet?

The battle of the skins of red wine?

This diversion had eaten up a few miles and quite a few minutes but, as he had told Ben, he had to sort it all out. He hadn't done that yet.

A horn blared and he jerked the car toward the shoulder realizing he had been speeding down the middle of the highway.

He might never be able to sort it out but in that instant he knew what he was going to do.

Turn around. Stop at the little coffee place he frequented and pick up two cups. Black and hot. They get you up at early dawn in hospitals so Sydney was certain to be awake.

When you can corner her she's a good listener. He had to tell her what he was going to do. She must know that he had suspected something sinister for a long while. He had not been comfortable with what Santiago was doing. The fast car, the elegant apartment in Madrid, the extravagant life style. It was not real. Why had he not questioned Santiago? Not asked for an explanation? Because he was afraid of the answer, he told himself solemnly as he turned back to Avila.

Sydney has been having a nightmare. Edna and the new Hugo were in her hospital room, only instead of jeans and a sleeveless shirt he was dressed as a priest. Edna was wearing a long black skirt and a shirt with a shawl around her shoulders.

She was choking. She couldn't breathe. Hugo was leaning across her body and she was struggling to push him away.

But this was no ordinary nightmare.

Edna nodded to Hugo. The shot had done its work.

"OK." She motioned him toward the door.

He was strong and it was easy for him to lift Sydney's limp body. The hospital gown slipped to one side and her long legs dangled, her bare feet almost touching the floor.

Edna signaled for him to wait as she eased the door open and scanned the hall. Following her directions he moved to the emergency exit. There were no more than six steps and he managed them in seconds.

"Stop."

He obeyed, responding to one of his few words in English. She eased past him and his burden and opening the door peered into the parking lot.

It was just daybreak and there was no one in sight as they drove away in the rented car.

"I have brought coffee for Señora Reardon." Peter Farber held up two paper cups. "Strong and black, just the way she likes it."

The nurse smiled and sent him down the hall.

It was amazing. In that moment when he pulled the car back to safety he knew exactly what he was going to do and he was eager to tell her.

"Sydney," he said softly as he pushed open the door. "Sydney," he repeated a bit louder as he entered. The bed was still in shadow. He crossed the room.

No one there. Empty!

"Sydney!" he almost shouted.

He checked the bathroom. He looked under the bed, which was ridiculous. He hurried to the nurses' station.

"Señora Reardon is not in the room."

"She must be. She was sleeping when I checked not an hour ago."

"She is not there. Call the police. Captain Marquez."

The captain was there in a matter of minutes. "I telephoned Ben Harris. He will come to my office." Before he caught himself

he admitted that he had seen no reason to post a guard. He had assumed Señora Reardon would be safe in the hospital.

"Why did you return?" he abruptly asked Peter Farber.

"I wanted to talk with Sydney. To tell her something."

"What did you plan to tell her?"

Farber considered his answer. "It was personal."

"I may need to ask the question again," Marquez said before he turned away. He looked over his shoulder. "Do you wish to come to police headquarters?"

"Yes, of course."

They had been at the station only a few minutes when Ben Harris burst into the room. "This is ridiculous! Incompetent. We persuaded Sydney to go to the hospital so she'd be safe." He threw up his hands. "What happened?"

"Hysterics will not help," Marquez said to Ben as if he were chiding an unruly child.

Ben sighed. "I know. What action do we take?"

"No action. We wait."

They had been waiting most of the morning when the switchboard operator summoned Captain Marquez.

He covered the receiver, motioning to the operator. *"Detenlo en el telefono."*

Ben could follow well enough to know that he was trying to keep the caller engaged long enough to trace the call.

The line went dead.

Marquez sighed. "Not enough time. They have the señora. They want ten million dollars."

"Could you identify the voice?"

"No. Frightened. The words ran together."

"What do we do now?" Ben asked.

"We wait," Marquez repeated patiently.

Sydney opened her eyes and turned her head slowly from side to side. She moved a foot and could feel warm sand and grass between her toes. An ant had crawled across her foot and was meandering up her leg. She should slap it but the mere thought was too taxing. A few feet away she could see heavy shoes topped by jeans. She leaned back against a tree and looked up.

"Edna?"

"Yeah. Sure took you a long time to wake up. I was about to think I give you too much."

It had not been a nightmare. She *had* seen Edna standing over her. She *had* been held down on the bed and felt the sting of a needle.

"Where's the new Hugo?" she asked inanely.

There was that gurgle that she recalled from the bizarre scene at the parador.

"He's gone to call the police."

"Call the police?"

"Yeah. To tell 'em we'll give you back for ten million."

"Ten million dollars?"

"That's what them stones you was carryin' are worth."

Sydney smiled apprehensively. "I'm sure the police won't think I'm worth that."

"That's what I'm afraid of. I should of just left you in the hospital. I thought the other Hugo would take you out and try to get all that money. I didn't want him to do that. Greed. The Bible speaks to that and I should of listened."

A car was approaching. "It's Hugo."

He came up to them fast and slammed on the brakes creating a cloud of dust. Throwing the keys on the seat he rushed to Edna leaving the car door ajar.

"Bastardos, les dije que diez millones por ella viva." He pointed at Sydney. *"No dijeron ni sí ni no. Quisieron detenerme en el telefono. Yo se."*

Edna summoned Sydney. "You speak Spanish?"

"A bit."

"Listen to him. What's he sayin'?"

Sydney tried to get up and found her knees weak. She tried again and managed to rise.

Hugo repeated what he had said. In his nervousness he hesitated, ran words together, then hesitated.

"He says he told the bastards you want ten million dollars for me to be returned. They didn't agree. He thinks they were trying to keep him on the telephone so they could trace the call."

"Anything else?"

"No."

Edna and Hugo walked away. She was still talking angrily in English. He was shouting just as feverishly in Spanish. Sydney heard him insisting, *"Matenla! Matenla ahora."*

Even not knowing Spanish, Edna could be pretty sure he wanted to kill Sydney now.

The car door was open just a few yards away, the keys on

the seat. Edna and Hugo were continuing their argument in English and Spanish. They were probably going to agree on killing her at some point so it was worth a try. Sydney scrambled into the car, put the keys in the ignition and rushed forward.

Hugo was incredibly fast. Bullets shattered the windshield. Edna was running toward the car, waving her arms. "Stop! Stop!"

She was not five feet away when Sydney braked.

"Jesus, I can't do it," she whispered and leaned on the steering wheel.

Edna was shaken but clearly puzzled. "Why didn't you run over me?"

"I couldn't. I couldn't run you down."

"Might of been a bad mistake." Edna pondered, shaking her head, probably the closest she had ever come to introspection. "Might of saved your life. Get out."

Hugo was still shouting.

"Go on," Edna screamed. Sensing her anger he walked away, kicking rocks in frustration.

"Get out," she repeated and Sydney reluctantly opened the car door.

"Why didn't you kill me when you could of?" She was still puzzling.

"I just couldn't."

"I would of killed you."

"I am most pleasantly surprised that you haven't yet."

"Pleasantly surprised! You're a cool one. Wish you was on my team."

"I have to know something. Those letters to the monastery. Who?" She faltered. "How?"

Edna was close to smiling. "Who wrote them since I'm so ignorant?"

114

Sydney started to protest.

"I'll tell you. I'll be long gone before you get to the police. Hugo killed both my boys. But I have a daughter. April. She was born in that month. The boys never had no interest in school. April wanted to learn everything. I saw to it she got through college. She's a whiz on those computers. She admires me because I work in nursing homes. Calls it merciful. Can you beat that?

"She sends me money ever once in a while. Ain't that thoughtful? When I needed letters for the relic I asked her. She was proud of me for doin' such a good thing. Once I got the letters havin' them look official was no problem. I know guys who can make anything official."

Edna walked away, thinking about what to do next. "Go on," she said peevishly when Hugo approached her. "Not now." He may not have understood the words but the intent was clear.

Exhausted by her effort to escape, Sydney slumped down under a tree.

Edna came over. "I've been thinkin'. About what to do with you. I didn't let Hugo kill you when I should of. The police ain't giving up ten million for you. If they did the bills would be marked anyway. So I'm goin' to leave you right here under this tree. You ain't goin' too fast with no shoes. I ain't even goin' to tie you up. Here's water." She threw a plastic bottle on the ground. "See I can be kind. I appreciate you not killin' me. But I want your word."

"My word? About what?"

"That you won't tell the police nothin' until after five hours. Shouldn't take that long to cross the border but I don't want to be pushed."

"Five hours? To get to the airport and leave the country?"

Edna gurgled. "Madrid maybe ain't the best way out. You're plenty smart. You figure it out."

"What time is it? Hugo took my watch."

"Little after noon. Five hours. Have I got your word?"

Sydney nodded.

Walking toward the car she added, "My daughter's name ain't really April and she don't do computers."

Watching Edna and Hugo disappear down the dusty, rutted road, Sydney pulled herself to her feet. The highway must be out there somewhere.

She ventured away from the shade. The sand was more than warm. The pebbles were abrasive.

"Start walking," she ordered herself.

After trudging for half an hour she still could not find the main road.

Her feet were stinging and beginning to bleed.

"I can't do it," she whispered. The landscape shimmered in the distance. "Jesus, this is what happens before you fall down and die. Don't be melodramatic," she finished aloud. "You can make it. Keep moving."

Had it been an hour, or hours, when she spotted a car speeding along the edge of the world in front of her?

It still seemed an eternity before she was standing on the side of the road waving as cars, trucks, and buses sped by.

A big, black Mercedes with tinted windows slowed and taking heart, she moved hopefully to the edge of the pavement.

At the last moment the driver accelerated.

Sydney waved. "I wouldn't pick me up," she acknowledged aloud to herself.

A decrepit truck pássed her. Stopped. Backed up.

Two suckling pigs tethered in the bed looked at her inquiringly as she rushed toward the cab.

"*¿Señora?*" the seamed, friendly face crinkled.

"*Por favor. Lleveme a Avila a la estación de policía.*"

"*¿A la estación de policía?*"

"*Sí. Les prometo que no estan en mingun peligro.*"

No wonder he was skeptical about taking her to the police. She did her best to explain that the police would be happy to see her and that he was in no peril for delivering her.

As Sydney was climbing in, the scruffy dog who had been occupying the passenger seat scrunched himself down on the floorboards and began sniffing her bloody feet. As the ancient vehicle jerked ahead she glanced down and could see asphalt blurred through cracks in the tired floor.

The old man looked over at her and smiled, revealing a single tooth in the middle of his upper gum.

"*Bueno. Buen perro.*"

She couldn't have agreed more. It was indeed a good, good dog.

"*¿Como se llama?*"

"*Perro. Es un amigo pero es perro.*"

Perro. Dog? That's not a name, it's a job description, she thought to herself, as the animal licked her damaged feet.

"*¿Cual es su nombre?*"

"*Ernesto Segovia.*"

"*Mi nombre es* Sydney Reardon. Are you taking the pigs to market"

He shrugged to indicate he did not understand the question.

"*¿Llevan los puercos al mercado?*"

"*Al parador. Los triago cada semana.*"

To the parador. What a small world. "*¿Al parador? Que mundo tan chico. Hay es donde estoy hospedada.*"

He nodded and smiled.

"*Gracias. Gracias,*" Sydney said as the truck faltered to a halt in front of the station.

"Goodbye. Thank you *Perro.*" She petted the dog as she stepped down.

Ben Harris was laughing and pointing to Sydney, standing in the doorway of the police station barefoot and wearing only a hospital gown.

"Sydney, you look absurd," he snickered.

"That's enough," Farber snapped. He removed his jacket and drew Sydney into the room. Draping the coat around her shoulders, he realized that it did not really protect her from the indignity of the inadequate gown and her bare feet.

"Wow. You look wonderful, and dreadful, and ridiculous," Ben said as he went to hug her. "I'm just so relieved to see you. I think I lost it and started to laugh to keep from crying. Please. Forgive me."

"Señora," Marquez sighed. "You are with us." He placed a chair near her and gestured for her to sit. "Who held you prisoner? Where were you? How did you escape? Where are your captors now?"

Even he could be surprised and flustered.

"What time is it?" Sydney asked.

"It is . . ." Finding the question completely out of context, Marquez looked at her questioningly. "It is almost a little after six o'clock."

Sydney then told them the whole saga. Even the bargain to not go to the police for five hours.

Marquez was pacing. He frowned. "Señora, if you agreed, that is obstructing justice. Why such a long time? They could be on a flight out of Madrid in half that time."

"I asked the same question. She said Madrid might not be the best way out. She told me I was smart, I could figure it out. I thought about it a good bit as I was walking, trying to keep my mind off my painful feet. My hunch is they went to Portugal."

"Would you have kept your word about the five hours?"

Sydney smiled the best she could with her swollen, bruised face. "Since more than five hours have elapsed, I'll never have to answer that question will I."

Marquez was not satisfied but he could only shrug. "How did you get here?"

"Not easily. After I finally reached the main road no one would pick me up. Can you blame them?" She stretched out her feet and made a sweeping gesture with her hands from head to toe. "Finally a toothless old man in a rickety truck stopped. He was taking two pigs to the parador."

Sydney began to sob.

"Captain," Peter said quickly. "Let us take Señora Reardon to the parador."

"Of course." He held the door as Farber helped Sydney into the back seat. "We may need to talk later."

Peter nodded. "You drive," he instructed Ben, handing him the keys. With a long comforting arm around Sydney's shoulders he was half murmuring, half humming, a reassuring sound.

"Sorry," Sydney whispered.

"Don't worry. You're going to have a soothing bath, get into some reasonable clothes, rest a bit and we'll bring you a light supper." With his free hand Peter tapped Ben on the shoulder. "And, if there's a bottle of Johnny Walker Black in this town we'll find it."

"We did find Johnny Walker Black." Peter held up the bottle as he entered Sydney's room.

Ben Harris followed carrying a small tub of ice and three glasses.

"Feeling better?" Peter asked. "At least you're looking better."

"Much better," Sydney acknowledged, leaning comfortably on pillows arranged against the head of the bed. "I can hardly wait for that Johnny Walker and learning what has happened since I disappeared."

"Soup, salad, and good bread will be along but while we savor our drinks here's what has happened."

Ben passed glasses around. "The old Hugo, as you refer to him, is dead."

"Santiago killed him," Peter added softly.

"Santiago killed him?"

"Well, in a sense." Farber cradled his head in his hands and barely paused as he explained what had taken place.

"Oh Peter. I can't believe Santiago is gone. You loved him so much. Did you know he was in danger?"

"I can't believe it either. I blame myself. There were so

123

many indications that something was amiss. The too elegant apartment. The fancy car. Excessively expensive jewelry."

After a labored sigh he continued. "I haven't sorted it all out yet."

"Oh Peter," Sydney murmured again.

"What are you going to do?" Ben asked.

"You figured out about the ring that's stealing jewelry and we know Edna is the brains. But we haven't stopped them yet. I'm going to find Edna."

"Wow! How?"

"I'm going to take Santiago's Rolex. I'm going to have his huge diamond put in a new setting just in case Edna may have seen it. I'm going to put one of his flamboyant gold chains around my neck and, wearing a silk shirt and a cashmere jacket, I'm going to check in and out of nursing homes until I find her. Or, more likely, until she discovers me.

"I think I know where to begin. Just a week or so ago I read about posh hospitals and nursing facilities in Mexico. Palatial establishments with acres of manicured lawns, peacocks walking around, fountains, world-class dining rooms and lots of servants. Rich Mexicans wear expensive jewelry. Why else would Edna want a young Mexican for her new Hugo?"

"You may be right," Ben mused. He turned to Sydney. "You said she told old Hugo she had a new territory in mind that would make what they've done so far look puny."

Sydney nodded.

"If I'm wrong I'll change my territory until I find her."

"What a clever notion." Sydney smiled at him. "But what about the university and Salamanca?"

"Spain holds nothing for me now. I need your help."

"My help?"

124

"Yes. Tell me everything you can remember about Edna and the young Hugo. Not tonight," he added hastily. "Think about it and jot down notes. Physical description, mannerisms, anything that will help me identify them."

"I remember quite a lot about them," she said ruefully. "You may be sure I'll make notes." Sipping her drink with pleasure, she looked at Ben. "Now you can go on with your pursuit of Don Q."

"I'm going to La Mancha tomorrow if you're OK and Marquez will let me leave town." He sat on the foot of the bed. "Come with me."

"No thank you luv. I'm going to be quiet and try to sort things out like Peter. I told you I sometimes have trouble with reality. I may sit in the shade and re-read *Don Quixote.*"

She smiled a little sadly. "Obviously my body needs rest but my mind does too. I'm having trouble remembering. I can't recall the name of the man who tossed me off a balcony in London. We were friends for years. I danced with him, laughed with him, slept with him now and then."

"His name is Ian Hardwick," Ben supplied. "And I hope he's going to be locked up for a long while. Would you like me to stay around for a bit?"

"No, but thank you for asking. In addition to resting and reading I'll be busy. Mother Mary Henriette said they don't have a fax machine. I'm going to get one for them. And I'm going to find a better truck for that nice Mr. Segovia who gave me a ride."

They were just finishing supper when Peter smiled affectionately at Sydney. "I must be getting back to Salamanca. I'll keep in touch."

"Peter, be careful. What you are planning is admirable but dangerous. Edna is frightening. Please be careful."

125

Farber leaned down and kissed Sydney lightly on the top of her head. "To quote Ben's favorite author, 'A woman's counsel is bad, but he who doesn't take it is mad.'"

After Peter left, Ben refilled their glasses.

"Now that these deadly days are over I'm looking forward to going on with research for my play."

"I shan't offer to return to the theatre to star in your play. There aren't many good roles for women in *Don Quixote*. I'm too old to play Dulcinea and too vain to be the housekeeper." She laughed. "But I'll come to see it."

"Promise?"

"Promise."

Edna pointed across the dam and the canyon. "Portugal."

She signaled for Hugo to park the car off to the side of the road.

"*Se nos quebró el coche*," Hugo explained as the border guards checked their passports. The two men had been drinking coffee and playing cards. They had little interest in a disabled car.

One of them pointed in response to Hugo's question about where they could catch a bus. He guided Edna from the border station across the road.

"*Buenas tardes.*"

"*Buenas tardes.*"

The driver stood up and helped the old woman board.

"*Gracias.*" Hugo took Edna's hand and led her along the aisle.

The driver watched in the rear view mirror over his head as the young priest gently settled the little woman into a seat.

He crossed himself.

Steering the big bus back to the pavement he smiled, thinking how good it is that there are still young ones, so kind and thoughtful, and wishing to serve God and man.

127